CLUSTERF*@K

LIFE SUCKS #4

ELISE FABER

CLUSTERF*@K
by Elise Faber

Copyright © 2021 ELISE FABER

Newsletter sign-up

CLUSTERF*@K
Copyright © 2021 ELISE FABER
Print ISBN: 978-1-63749-009-9
eBook ISBN: 978-1-63749-008-2
Cover Art by Jena Brignola

LIFE SUCKS SERIES

1

CLUSTERF*@K

Misty

THE OCEAN DIDN'T GIVE a damn about her woes.

Too bad it couldn't wash them away as effectively as it conquered the sandcastle the kids had spent hours building.

All that remained now was a mound of sand, one that was disappearing more by the second.

And in the distance, the sky was just beginning to grow darker.

She was sitting on the deck of the cottage—belonging to Soph, her friend and sister-in-law, and her brother, Rob—enjoying the cool breeze whipping her hair, the sun on her skin, and a moment of quiet from the party still raging on the sand. Raging, if one could consider building epic sandcastles and running from the waves, with a couple of hard seltzers in hand, raging.

Which Misty did.

That was what all the wild knitters did.

And crocheters because she did that, too.

And—

Soph had just announced she was pregnant.

So that was more exciting than castles and waves.

Mainly because Misty was so happy for Soph and Rob, so glad they'd found each other and managed to carve out a slice of joy. Rob had been a widower, pretending to be happy and fulfilled. Soph had been—still was—a successful actor and equally successful at pretending all was good. They'd fallen for each other. They'd struggled. They'd figured things out.

They were perfect for each other, and—

It was just...Misty was jealous.

So *freaking* jealous.

And add in a dash of guilt. Because her brother had barely survived the death of his first wife, had been a shell of a man for two full years until Sophie had come into the picture in her sexy little heels, with her Hollywood smile and her sweet personality.

Yup. Soph was a famous actor.

And she was *nice*.

Ugh. If Misty didn't love Sophie so much, she'd hate her.

Sighing, knowing that probably didn't make sense, she sat back and lifted her glass of wine to her lips, glugging down a large sip and looking out at the surf. Of all the places to live in town, her brother certainly had picked a good one.

Even if she was a jealous, guilty asshole.

She had her own business. She'd bought a house. She'd just paid off her car. She had a full life.

A full—of yarn—single, *lonely* life.

Fun, fun.

Resisting the urge to sigh again, she drained her glass then made her way over to say goodbye to her brother and Soph and the rest of the crew.

"Oh," Soph said, after Misty had made her excuses. "I was hoping you might stay around. My dad and brothers are coming to visit." She checked her watch. "They're actually supposed to be here any minute."

"I have an early morning delivery," Misty lied. "I'm sorry. I really need to get to bed."

"I understand." Soph squeezed her hands. "I'll make dinner this week on a night you can join us. Friday? You don't have classes then, right?"

"Right." A beat. That was five days from then. Misty would be over her jealous, guilty self by then.

Right?

Definitely.

Misty forced a smile. "Friday is great."

She waved to her friend Finn, who was cradling his new baby, high-fived his daughter Rylie (master sandcastle extraordinaire), and called a goodbye to Shannon, Finn's wife, then she high-tailed it back across the sand, determined to allow herself one more night of sulking before she got it together and stopped feeling so sorry for herself. She would wake up in the morning and be over her jealous, guilty self, so that by the time Friday dinner rolled around with her brother and Soph, she would be nothing but happy for them.

She'd make sure of that, even if it was just faking it until she made it.

Plus, Misty had a lot going for her.

She just needed to remember that.

And she would.

Tomorrow.

After she finished the bottle of wine in her fridge and the pint of ice cream in her freezer. After she'd lit her favorite candle and soaked in her tub, consuming bad reality TV right alongside all those extra calories.

"See?" she whispered to herself as she got into her car and turned on the engine, shifting into reverse as she backed out of the driveway. "This will all be fi—"

Crunch.

Her sedan—her awesome, recently-paid off sedan—jerked to a halt.

"Fuck," she whispered, looking in her review and seeing that she'd run into a large black SUV. An SUV that currently had smoke coming from beneath the hood. She cursed again, dropping her head to the steering wheel for a moment, before sighing and pushing out of her car.

"I'm sorry," she began as the driver's door on the SUV opened. "I didn't see you—"

The rest of her words froze in her throat as tall, dark, and handsome got out of said SUV.

He was the sexiest man she'd ever seen in her life, bar none. Towering at least a foot over her and with broad shoulders encased in tight black cotton, he had a thick black beard, piercing green eyes, and a smile that sucker-punched her right in the gut.

"There," she finished.

He lifted a brow, still smiling. "Obviously."

"I'm sorry," she said again. "I—"

He took a step toward her, those green eyes kind. "It's fine. It's just a car. Look, I—"

"It's not fine," she told him, waving her hands at the SUV. "Look at your car. Look what I *did!*" Unbidden, tears stung the backs of her eyes, and she blinked rapidly. It was an accident. She wouldn't cry. She *couldn't* cry over something she clearly hadn't meant to do. That would be absolutely ridiculous.

But this was the nail in the coffin on her emotions, and she was a crier under normal circumstances. Under these? Riddled with guilt and running into the hottest guy in the universe's SUV? Making smoke pour out from beneath the hood?

This was *certainly* an accident that she would cry over.

She was a jealous jerk and single and lonely and alone—yes, she knew that lonely and alone were basically the same thing—but she supposed it was possible to be lonely while actually being around other people. And that also shouldn't be what she was thinking about right now. Not with tears threatening, and not with the fact that she now needed to add shitty driver to her list of jealous, single, lonely, *and* alone.

A finger on her cheek, wiping away a tear that had escaped. "Don't cry, honey."

She sniffed. Another tear slipped free. He wiped it away.

He stepped closer, and she was inundated by his scent. Warm like the sun, spicy like the cayenne that she liked to add to her homemade artichoke and spinach dip. "What's your name?"

"Misty Hansen," she whispered.

Recognition in those green eyes. "Rob's sister."

She nodded, though it hadn't been phrased as a question.

"Hi, Misty." He waited until she met his gaze. "I'm Chance —" His eyes broke away from hers. "Oh, shit." He jerked, started running past her.

She turned to see what he was looking at.

Turned to see what he was too late to do anything about.

Her car—her freshly paid-off, awesome sedan was rolling forward...right into her brother's garage door.

Crunch.

Fuck. Her. Life.

"Jackson," he finished, looking back at her with wide green eyes.

2

TIGER'S EYES

Chance

SHE WAS BEAUTIFUL, albeit a bad driver.

Long blond hair trailing down her back, pretty brown eyes that swirled with different shades of russet and gold and tawny, reminding him of that gemstone, tiger's eye, a curvy body, lush lips, and…an expression that tugged at his heartstrings. She'd been crying before, tears slowly dripping down her face. *This—*

She was going to lose it.

"Hey," he said, moving toward her. "It's okay—"

"It's not okay," she began, words hitching on a sob. "I'm so—"

"Misty!" Rob, his sister's husband, tore around the corner, his face a mask of concern. "Are you okaaay…?" He finished the question on a long, drawn out breath, his gaze going from Chance's car to Misty's to his now crunched-in garage door.

"Rob," Misty said, rubbing her cheeks, and Chance watched with no little amount of respect as she straightened her shoulders, took a breath, and locked down the tears, as she walked over to Rob and said calmly, "I'm so sorry. I—" She broke off, and Chance waited to see what she would say. Would she try to minimize the clusterfuck that had just happened?

Or would she own up?

"It's a long story," she went off after a jerk of her head. "Or well, not long, but it all happened really fast, but I didn't see Chance pulling in, and I backed into his SUV, and then I got out and"—a wince that pulled her brows together—"I guess I didn't put my car into park because it rolled forward and"—white teeth pressed into her bottom lip—"well, unfortunately for your nice, new house, um...your garage door happened to be in the way."

Chance snorted.

She shot him a glare, no sign of those tears, then turned back to Rob, sighing. "I'm really sorry. I'll pay to have it repaired." Her gaze drifted back to Chance's. "Your car, too."

Silence.

From Rob.

Chance, on the other hand, was very close to losing it. Not because he was pissed, but because this was a disaster that could only be handled with laughter. Only, neither Rob nor Misty looked like they would be ready to laugh anytime soon.

Rob, probably because this was a brand new house and the front of it was sporting some serious damage.

Misty, probably because she was embarrassed, as any human would be based on the last five minutes.

She took it well, again, though. Just lifted her chin, moved to her car, and carefully reversed it away from the garage. It looked worse once the sedan was out of the way. Maybe the door was cheap, or maybe her car was heavier than it appeared. Either way, the garage door had a decent-sized dent in it, along with the wooden siding to the right of it. The door was probably fucked. The siding and house were going to need some work, and not all of that work would be cosmetic.

He noted that this time, she triple-checked that the car was in park before getting out.

With a stack of papers in her hand, she crossed over to him. "You have your phone?" she asked.

Chance lifted his brows.

"You can take a picture of my insurance information."

His lips twitched, and he pulled his cell from his pocket, snapped a pic then held it out toward her.

Now *her* brows lifted.

He closed her fingers around it. "Put your number in there in case I need to get ahold of you."

Those brows remained lifted, but suspicion had joined the ranks.

Probably because some of the humor and attraction he felt for her was bleeding into his face. She was cute. She owned her shit. She'd swallowed her tears.

Yeah, this was a cool chick.

"About the cars," he added when she didn't immediately take the cell.

Slowly, her brows descended. "Right," she murmured, plugging in her number, and he fought another chuckle—along with a blip of disquiet since he tended to stay away from women who were cool and might make a place in his heart and instead focused on those that were easy (easy to leave, easy to keep at a distance)—when he saw the disappointment in her eyes. He'd noticed her, thought she was fucking gorgeous, bad driving or not, but she'd also noticed him.

Which meant this was going to be fun.

Or disastrous.

Or...*no*, fun. He always made things fun.

"Can you move your car?" she asked, just as Soph came around the corner and gasped.

He watched pink spill on to Misty's cheeks, her shoulders slump slightly...then a little further when several more people rounded the house—a good-looking man, a beautiful woman with deep brown skin and shocking blue eyes, a little girl whose mouth went from smiling to shocked.

Misty groaned quietly.

"What happened?" the little girl asked.

Silence. Then Misty spoke up. "It was my fault." Her gaze went to Soph's. "I'm sorry. I'll pay to get it fixed."

Soph was his sister—by heart rather than blood—and she was also a famous actor.

She didn't need Misty to pay to repair the garage, accident or not.

And she made him proud by striding across the driveway, slipping an arm around Misty's waist, and saying quietly enough so no one besides him and Misty could hear, "You absolutely will *not* be paying to repair this. Shit happens. Plus"—she smiled and gently jostled Misty—"my man happens to be a contractor *and* your brother. He'll get it sorted."

Misty groaned again and dropped her head on to Soph's shoulder, and it did something to Chance's heart to see his sister, so easily accepting the touch, so easily *initiating* it.

She'd been through hell.

He still remembered how tiny and broken she'd been when she'd first moved in with them. To see her out in the world, whether as an actor pretending to be someone else, or just a friend, but seeing her as a woman in a loving relationship was nearly a miracle. And he was so damned proud of how far Soph had come.

"I'm paying," Misty said firmly, proving that she had spine.

Chance liked spine. Chance liked lush curves and long blond hair he could sink his hands into.

He'd like both more if they didn't belong to the sister of the man his *own* sister was seeing, but if Misty was interested, *he* was interested, family complications aside.

Life was too short to worry about complications.

Plus, he'd make it fun for them both while it lasted, and then he'd leave her happy while they remained friends.

That was how he rolled.

Leave 'em with a smile and fond memories, but always leaving them.

Because it was better for both of them that way.

Except, seeing Rob come up to Soph, placing his palm over her stomach in a way that was both tender and loving and revealed the news his family was gathering to hear made him wonder if it was really better.

But since that was an uncomfortable thought that had him thinking about things he really didn't like to think about, Chance shoved it down, focused on the trio, and watched the show.

"You're not paying," Soph countered.

Rob nodded in agreement.

Misty started to argue, but then Rob said, "You're not."

"I am—"

"Not," Rob repeated.

"I'm—" She broke off with a sigh and rubbed her forehead. "We can talk about this later," she said. "I really do need to get home."

"Dewdrop," Rob murmured.

Chance's heart squeezed but even more so when Misty's eyes went glassy again, her bottom lip trembling as she looked away from her brother and right toward him.

She blew out a breath.

But it felt like she'd exhaled some sort of magical mist, because he felt exposed, vulnerable, wanting to take her in his arms in a way that was less fun and more comforting.

Then she blinked and the tears were gone. The trembling lip stabilized.

Chance felt himself stabilize, too, the sensation in his chest disappearing just as quickly, and it was almost easy to pretend it hadn't been there in the first place.

Soph squeezed her arm. "You sure you're okay?"

A snort, her shoulders straightening. "I should be asking

you that. I'm not the one with the broken garage 'cause her sister-in-law can't drive."

"Babe," Soph said. "It's okay. Go home and get some sleep. We'll deal with this in the morning."

Misty nodded, threw her arms around Soph. "I really am so sorry."

Soph hugged her tight then pulled back and studied her face, concern rippling through Soph's eyes. "You're not okay."

"I'm fine." But she didn't sound fine, even as she turned and hugged Rob. Misty sounded very far away from fine. Soph didn't push, though, or maybe she didn't have time because Misty finished hugging her brother, who returned to the garage to continue his inspection, then rotated toward Chance and asked again if he could move his car.

Chance nodded, rubbing his chest in a way that he was trying to pretend didn't speak to something changing in his heart (fun, just fun!) and backed up his SUV, the grinding and hissing sounds as it moved not instilling a lot of confidence in its ability to cart him around. Still, he made sure to pull it well out of the way before watching Misty reverse at a snail's pace out of the driveway, inching back and checking for traffic no less than half a dozen times, even though there was minimal traffic on the street.

Minimal but not none, hence his unhappy front bumper.

Then she was gone, and he'd parked in her place—making sure it was actually *in* park—and moved toward his sister. She hugged him tight then pulled back and studied his eyes for several long moments. "I don't know if I should give you her number and tell you to go for it, or if I should warn you to stay the hell away." A beat. "She's special, Chance. Not temporary. She's a forever woman."

There was that gut punch again.

Or maybe a heart punch.

Because the vulnerability was back.

But he injected a bit of cocky into his tone anyway, tried to play it off as though it was all business as usual. "I already got her number."

Soph's brows shot up in surprise, and then she sighed. "Don't fuck it up."

He wouldn't.

Namely because he never allowed himself to get close enough to a woman in the first place to fuck it up.

Fun. Fucking. Friends.

That trifecta worked for him.

And Misty, as lush and pretty and with plenty of spine as she was, would be no different.

3

TOTALED

Misty

SHE WAS RESEARCHING BODY SHOPS.

After having spent nearly an hour on the phone with her insurance company.

And after having spent several hours of the early morning reaching out to contractors and garage door specialists.

Yes, her brother was a contractor.

No, he shouldn't have to clean up the fucking mess she'd made of the front of his house.

So, she'd take her lunch break to meet with one company, and then would meet the contractor bright and early the next morning. And she would be footing the bill. No matter what Soph said.

Her fault.

Her wallet.

The latter of which was going to be a lot lighter, but that was karma for her. Next time she'd double-check for traffic. Or maybe triple-check. Or...

The bell above the door rang, and she glanced up to see her two best friends Frankie—short for Francesca—and Mags—

short for Maggie. The grins on their faces didn't bode well for her future. Neither did Maggie sidling up to the counter, leaning a hip against it, and slowly closing Misty's laptop. "What's this about you careening into tall, dark, and handsome?"

She opened her laptop on a wince. "I didn't career. It was more…reversing at a regretful speed."

"Regretful?" Frankie asked, having arrived at the counter a moment after Maggie. She'd detoured to check out Misty's new display of yarn (because it was colorful and pretty, and Frankie loved yarn as much as Misty did). "How could speed be regretful?"

"When it's paired with a sedan reversing at the right"—or wrong, she supposed—"angle to crunch into the front bumper of an SUV that was twice its size."

Now Frankie and Maggie both winced. "That bad?"

Misty nodded. "It was hissing and releasing steam, and when he tried to move it, the noise was… well, akin to a plethora of rusty nails screeching against metal."

"Yikes," Frankie murmured.

Maggie whistled and brushed her hands together but then almost immediately straightened, clearly ready to move on from Misty's bad driving with nary a second thought—as was her way. Mags was an easy-come-easy-go kind of person. She didn't get stressed about things like car accidents or storms coming up the shore. A broken heel? Missing a sale at the Kate Spade outlet and not getting her fix for her latest sparkly wallet? *Those* things had Mags losing her shit. But Misty feeling like an idiot because she hadn't checked traffic and then more of one because she hadn't put her car in park (seriously, what the fuck was wrong with her?), that was easy to move on from.

"Well," Maggie said, drifting over to a pair of glittery knitting needles, drawn like a magpie to all the shiny. "Your first accident took until you were thirty. That's pretty good."

Frankie nodded. "That's true. But she's only twenty-nine, Mags."

The bell tinkled, and Misty glanced toward the door, an automatic reaction honed from her multiple years in business.

Only this time, it wasn't a woman, as was typical—though not always, since she did have a few male knitters, and Rob, knitting skills aside, visited quite often. This time it was a man —a tall, dark, and handsome man.

Chance Jackson.

"Fuck," she whispered.

His gaze drifted around the store, rested on her, and he smiled, started to come over.

Mags whipped toward her, eyes wide. "Is that him?" she whispered, which wasn't really a whisper, since Mags, in her easy-come-easy-go demeanor, didn't tend to pay attention to things like the volume of her voice. "Oh, please Jesus, tell me that's tall, dark, and handsome."

"Of course, that's him," Frankie said, much more quietly than Mags. "He looks like Soph."

"Actually, Soph is adopted," Misty murmured out of the corner of her mouth. "But yes, that's him, and also, please, kill me now." She raised her voice as he got close, though his smile told her he'd heard every bit of their conversation. "Chance, so good to see you again."

He paused, gaze on hers, the corners of his mouth just barely tipping up, though those green eyes danced. "It's good to see you, too."

There was a beat tagging along at the end of that statement, as though he'd swallowed the second half of it, and she could imagine what he was thinking of saying. ("It's good to see you, too, especially not behind the wheel of a car that's slamming into mine.") Luckily, her friends didn't give her too much time, not when Mags was sidling close and unleashing her full-wattage smile, the one that often left even Misty a bit muddled by proxy, even though it was only wielded on the male populace.

"Chance, is it?" she said. "How long are you in town?" (*Read: Can we boink?*) She rested her hand on his chest, just for a heartbeat. "Oh, wow. That's some muscle."

Misty dropped her head back, stared up at the ceiling.

She loved Mags. She really did.

But her friend was a bit much.

Sighing, she lifted her head, seeing that Chance wasn't even looking at Mags, despite the chest touch. His eyes were focused on her, and there was heat in their depths that had her stomach going squishy.

Girding her loins, she forced a smile. "Chance, this is my best friend, Maggie." She nodded at her voluptuous, brunette, troublesome friend. "And"—a nod at Francesca—"this is my other best friend, Frankie."

He nodded at both of them, barely glancing their way, even though they were gorgeous and had gotten more than their fair share of second-looks, but he didn't say anything, just returned his eyes to her and kept staring with that heat in his deep green eyes.

"I—" She stopped. "Can I help you with something?"

"Yes."

Misty waited.

He just kept staring.

Mags stepped back, drawing Misty's focus. She saw that her friend's brows were lifted, and there was amusement written in the lines of her face. Amusement along with an unwritten push for Misty to be the one doing the chest touching with Chance, because based on his focus, he'd be more receptive to Misty doing it over Mags and...well, as previously mentioned, Mags was easy-come-easy-go. Chance wasn't interested—even with the smile and chest touch—so she was moving on. "We'll go look at...*something*."

Frankie, shy sometimes to a fault, shook her quiet off and

wove her arm through Maggie's. "I saw some yarn I think you'll like."

"Right. Yarn," Mags said. "And those glittery needles."

Then she tugged Frankie off to the far end of the shop.

Note: they were neither near the glittery knitting needles, nor the yarn. They were shamelessly staring at her by the small selection of knitting baskets she kept in stock.

Also note: they weren't out of earshot, since her store wasn't that big, though they were far enough away that they'd have to concentrate to hear whatever Chance had to say to her.

Never fear, though, they *would* be concentrating.

Once they'd reached the corner, Misty returned her attention to Chance. He was still and silent, studying her, making her nerves prickle and goose bumps lift on her arms. "I, um"—she opened her computer—"I've been researching body shops. Todd at A-1 on First Street said that he could look at your car this afternoon—"

He lifted a hand. "No need."

"Oh," she said, biting her lip, "you already got it in somewhere?"

The man must work fast. Though she'd spent hours on the phone that morning, not getting *her* car to the shop, so he'd probably been more efficient than her, especially since he wasn't searching for contractors and garage door repairmen alongside that.

He shrugged. "I had a buddy come look at it last night. It's totaled. Put in an order for a new one. It'll be here this afternoon."

She was still processing the first part of his statement when the second penetrated.

"Totaled?" she sputtered.

Oh shit.

"*Ordered?*" She shook her head sharply. He'd ordered a car? Like it was an item off a menu, or a book off Amazon? How? What—

Also, how in the fuck was she going to pay him for a brand-new car?

She didn't have that kind of money.

She barely had enough to pay her own deductible.

Fuck. *Fuck.* Her hands clenched into fists at her sides.

"Misty."

"I—um—" She closed her eyes then straightened her shoulders and sighed, lids peeling back so she could meet his green ones. A nod. "Right. I'll figure out a way to pay you for the car." And pay for the garage door and the wall and *her* car and—

"It's covered."

She blinked. "What?"

"I'm not here about the car. That's between me and my insurance company—"

"Um—" It also involved her and *her* insurance company.

"Misty," he said again.

"I promise, I'll speak to them and—"

"It's covered."

"It can't possibly be covered," she said. "I spent hours on the phone with my agent this morning, and I barely got a commitment for an adjuster to come out. That doesn't even count me having to look up body shops and—"

"*It's covered,*" he repeated. For a third time.

"But...how?" She was nowhere *near* covered, and her issues were only with her bumpers. Chance's engine had been smoking and hissing, and now he'd ended up with a new car and—

Half his mouth curved up. "Sounds like your insurance sucks, babe. I sent some pictures. I talked to my agent. Adjuster came out this morning, and since my SUV is totaled, there's no need to dick around."

Fingers clenching on the counter to keep her upright, she squeaked out for the second time, "Totaled?"

The other half of his mouth tipped. "You've got good aim, babe. Bent the frame. No coming back from that."

Now she wavered on her feet.

Fuck. *Fuck.* This was so much worse than she'd expected... and she'd spent the night rehashing, so thus had expected some serious shittiness.

Now, she needed to pay for a new SUV.

"I'll pay you back," she began, fully aware she was spiraling, yet unable to stop herself. She was the responsible one of her friend group. She had always made sure they didn't get in trouble, whether it was getting home tipsy from a high school party to freezing Maggie's credit card in a block of ice so she didn't buy yet another pair of ankle boots she didn't need. "I can do"—Misty did some mental tabulation—"nine hundred today, and I'll figure out how to get the rest and—"

Her words cut off this time because he was in her space.

Like *seriously* in her space.

One second, he'd been on the other side of the counter. The next, he was *there.* Spinning her so she faced him, his hands on either side of her, resting on the glass, boxing her in, his spicy scent overwhelming her senses, the heat from his body soaking through the light sweater she'd knitted like it was a hot knife coasting through butter.

"I *said,* it's covered."

Firm words.

One might even say they were *hard* words, his eyes flashing with just a bit of annoyance. Well, he could be annoyed all he wanted. She'd fucked up, and she didn't shirk her responsibilities. Thus, Misty sucked in a breath and pressed on. "It can't be covered," she said, watching them flash again, a lightning storm among gleaming emeralds. "Even if your insurance company will cut a check, it won't be for what it's worth." She knew about these things, knew that the moment a car was driven off the dealer's lot, the value dropped, and this played into the valuation the insurance company was going to make. His SUV had looked nice and new, and there was no way he wouldn't be in the hole after ordering a new one like it was a fucking pizza.

And yes, she was aware in some distant part of her brain that she was *still* spiraling.

But he talked about getting a new car like he'd ordered *a pizza*!

So no, she wouldn't just drop this.

She'd make things right.

Somehow, fuck somehow, she'd need to make this right.

4

IT'S COVERED

Chance

HE WAS LOSING HER.

He'd have to be an idiot to not see that.

And he might be a lot of things, but he didn't make a habit out of being an idiot.

"Hey," he said, dropping his hand to the side of her neck and finding his words colliding against each other in his throat, stumbling and tripping together and bottling up. Because her skin was like silk. Because she smelled like coconut. Because her eyes were even more beautiful up close. The varying shades of brown and gold all swirling together, sucking him in like a black hole.

She shuddered out a breath, and he smelled coffee and mint and something else that was deeper, a scent lingering on her skin that was floral.

Jasmine maybe?

Hibiscus?

Either way, it was intoxicating, and he found himself bending his head, pressing his nose to her neck, and inhaling deeply.

Another shudder, and he felt her arms start to come around him, her fingertips grazing his waist.

"Um," she breathed.

He flicked out his tongue, tasted her.

Fucking heaven.

"Come out with me."

She stiffened, and begrudgingly, he lifted his head. Not his arms, though. He kept those on the counter, caging her in. Mostly because he liked being there, but also because, based on the conversation from two minutes ago, she had a tornado of thoughts in her brain, thoughts she didn't need to have because he truly didn't give a shit about his car, and those thoughts were going to get in the way of him getting this woman in his bed.

He needed her in his bed.

He needed to see what those eyes did when he made her come.

He needed fun, fucking, and friends.

"What does that mean?" she asked, her brows pulling together and forming a V.

Fuck, she was cute. "It means you and me go to dinner, maybe a movie. We talk and sit close, hold hands, maybe you let me taste that luscious mouth of yours, and we see where that takes us."

Her lips parted, but he couldn't tear his gaze from her eyes. They'd gone molten, the gold streaks blazing, and he knew she felt it, too.

The pull.

The draw that was making his cock twitch.

Then she blinked, and the heat was gone. She pushed at his arm, tried to slide sideways away from him. He just let his hips fall forward, to rest more heavily against hers, and yeah, his cock twitched again. But he ignored it, studying her face and wondering where the tornado in her brain would take them next.

"I can't go out with you."

He grinned.

"*I can't,*" she repeated.

Unperturbed, he asked, "Why, babe?"

Her chin came up, and he had an intense urge to kiss it. So, he did. Probably not the best decision in this moment, but she was there and smelling of hibiscus and mint and coffee and coconut, and he didn't think, just pressed his lips to that adorable chin.

And maybe flicked his tongue out to taste her.

Fucking. Heaven.

Her fingers lifted, brushed his waist again. "Because I can't."

He lifted his gaze, but only enough to see her eyes. "Why?"

Her lips parted, breath hissing out and coating his. "Because I crashed into your car and totaled it, and I still need to pay you back because I know it hit your wallet, even if you keep saying *it's covered,*" she said in a fair approximation of his voice.

"It *is* covered," he told her, adding so she could protest, "Why else?"

"Because your Soph's brother, and Soph and *my* brother are together."

"Who cares?"

Her eyes widened, and fuck, she was pretty, especially when a flush of irritation turned her cheeks pink. "Who *cares?*" She shoved at his arm again and when that didn't budge him, she tossed up her hands. Chance shifted so that when they came down, they dropped onto his shoulders and—hip to hip, hands on his body, lips close—fuck, that was good. Even if she was too pissed to process their closeness...or all that goodness. "*Who cares?*" she exclaimed. "*I* care. Rob is not just my brother. He's been like a father to me. He picked up the pieces when our parents died. He held us together even when Carmella died"— Chance knew that was Rob's deceased wife—"and he's good and happy and finally whole again. I will not *fuck* that up."

"So," Chance said, lifting a hand and stroking a thumb

across one swathe of pink on her cheek and then the other, "we won't fuck it up."

Misty's eyes widened; her fingers dug in sharply. He shifted, because the woman had some grip, and then her gaze slid to her hands, her lips parted, and her grip immediately loosened, dropping her hands to her sides. "I'm sorry," she breathed. "I—"

He picked up her hands, put them back on his shoulders. "Next time, do that when we're both naked."

More pink.

"Uh—"

"Come out with me."

Hazed desire in those eyes, but she shook her head. "I—"

The bell above the door rang.

Misty spun and faced whoever had come in.

This had the pleasurable effect of positioning her ass between his thighs. "Do *this* while we're both naked, too."

She gasped, but her hips rocked back, rolling into his cock, which was definitely doing more than a twitch now. "I—" A shuddering sigh, her shoulders straightening, her body coming away from his. Then she cleared her throat, glared at him over her shoulder, and asked, "How can I help you, Mrs. Perkins?"

The old lady with short gray hair glanced from Chance to Misty to her friends pretending not to watch in the corner. Her brows lifted. Her smile was wide. "Frankie can help me," she said, bustling over to the display on the far side of the shop. "You two...carry on." A wave of her hand, her curious eyes drifting away only enough to navigate to the pair of women.

Who all bent together and began whispering.

Misty groaned, her back still to him.

He brushed her hair off her neck. "Should I say do *that* when you're naked, too?"

Her head dropped, chin resting on her chest. Then another sigh, her body going ramrod straight. "I'm not going out with you," she declared.

He pressed a kiss to the skin he'd exposed.

Then whispered in her ear. "Also, Soph already had a contractor at the house this morning. There's nothing more for you to do there."

She spun, eyes flashing "I said—"

A finger to her lips. "It's covered."

And then, eyes flashing, he turned for the door. "I'll pick you up Friday at seven."

"I'm busy."

Shit. He was, too. That was family dinner night at Soph and Rob's. Normally, he'd blow that off—not that he didn't love his family, but fun, fucking, friends—but he had the feeling Misty would be there at dinner, too.

So, he wouldn't be missing it.

"Saturday then."

"I—"

"Seven."

She stomped her feet, and he was left thinking that, fuck, she was cute again. "I'm not going out with you!"

He chuckled, his hand on the doorknob. "Saturday," he repeated.

He tugged open the door, started to step out, the bell tinkling overhead as he heard Mrs. Perkins exclaim loudly, "I don't know what you're thinking, Misty Hansen, but you'd better get your head straight. I'd give my left tit to go out with that man."

Barring hearing an old lady talk about her breasts, that was the funniest shit he'd heard in a long time.

But that wasn't what put the smile on his face as he walked through downtown and back to Rob and Soph's place.

Nope.

That was all Misty.

5

MALE LOGIC

Misty

HER BROTHER WAS TRYING to torture her.

He just didn't know it.

But there were five Jackson brothers around the table on his back deck, two Jackson parents, Soph, Rob, and her.

Dinner with Rob and Soph had turned into dinner with Rob, Soph, and all of Soph's family.

There was one Jackson brother who hadn't taken his eyes off her.

Two guesses who.

Stifling a snort, and knowing it would only take one, she straightened in her chair and refused to let her gaze drift back to Chance.

And failed.

But damn, he looked good.

He'd dressed up for dinner with the family, wearing a tight navy button-down with the sleeves rolled up to reveal tanned forearms and a tattoo that covered the inside of one arm, from wrist to elbow. She wasn't sitting close enough to see exactly what it was, but the urge to trace her fingers—and maybe her tongue—along the swirls of it was intense. As was the urge to bury her nose in the spot revealed by the open buttons of his shirt, to inhale the scent of him, to allow it to surround her like he had at her shop.

She'd dreamed of the fucker over the last four nights.

Then had woken each morning and had to bust into her collection of vibrators each of the last few mornings, while remembering the flick of his tongue on her skin, the press of his lips, the rough, sensual abrasion of his beard on her skin.

"Mist, you okay?"

Jumping and nearly upending her plate, she tore her gaze from Chance—fucking hell, *how* had it gotten back there?—and turned to look at Soph, who was trying to pass her a platter of food.

"Sorry," she said, taking it and shoveling food onto her plate so she didn't have to look at Soph, "my mind is other places."

"Is this about the garage door?" Soph asked quietly.

God, it would be so much easier if it was.

"No," she said, still scooping.

"About the wall?"

Also, no. Though those two items had been at the top of her list of worrying, along with the whole ordering-an-SUV thing. Another spoonful ended up on her plate. "No, Soph. I'm fine. Really. I mean, I do want to pay you back, but—"

"You know that's not an option."

Misty made a face.

"You can't argue with a pregnant woman."

Her face got...face-ier.

Soph studied her for a moment then smiled as she changed the subject, probably knowing she'd just won. "So, do you have any new patterns for me?"

"Of course, I do."

Soph was turning into quite an accomplished knitter, especially with all the downtime she had on set. She'd made her way through all the beginner patterns Misty had in stock and was now working on some intermediate ones.

"Great!" Her smile grew. "I'll come by tomorrow and if I time it right, we can grab lunch."

"Sounds great." And it did, until her eyes drifted across the table and found Chance's, remembering what he'd said about Saturday. Specifically, that he wanted to take her out. At seven. Because at that moment, *his* eyes seemed to say, "You'll go out with her, but not with me?"

Damn right, she would.

Soph wasn't complicated.

Not like Chance was.

Opening her mouth to say something, anything that would get her mind off all that complication, Misty was thwarted when Soph turned away and answered a question someone asked. Though Mist was too twisted up to pay attention to who asked it, especially when her gaze drifted back across the table, and she found herself falling fully into Chance Land.

True to his word, he had been right about Rob and Soph calling in the big guns. By the time she'd arrived during her lunch hour four days ago, the garage door had been replaced and the pillar was in the middle of being repaired. Her Yelp trolling had been for naught, which meant she had just needed to deal with her car.

Her car that had disappeared sometime between returning to her shop to finish out her day and teach her evening classes and stepping out her back door to the parking lot, only to find it empty.

Empty save Rob.

Who'd told her he'd taken it to the shop and to not give him lip—she had given him lip, anyway, because as much as he was her surrogate dad, he was still her brother, and she was used to taking care of herself. Once she'd gotten her ranting out of her system, he'd shoved her into his truck, driven her home, and zipped inside to make sure her newly finished bathroom was doing okay (long story, but the room was almost like their pet at this point—they'd had so many issues redoing it together that neither of them quite trusted that something else unexpected might not happen in there—more burst pipes or mold or a fucking poltergeist taking up residence and creating havoc). However, because his work was solid and her bathroom was now gorgeous, there wasn't much to check, so he'd kissed her on the forehead, told her he'd pick her up in the morning for work, reminded her about dinner Friday night, and then disappeared back to his Soph.

What he *hadn't* reminded her, and what she'd forgotten, was that dinner with him and Soph wasn't just dinner with him and Soph.

It was dinner with him, Soph, and all her family.

Five brothers. Her dad. Her mom.

That was fine. Misty owned a retail shop, for God's sake. She was good at small talk and charming people, and furthermore, Soph's family was nice and super cool.

The problem?

Chance staring at her like he couldn't wait to get into her fucking pants.

Her pants thinking that was a great idea.

And Rob, usually her barrier when it came to unwanted advances (*But is it unwanted?* her inner demon asked, knowing full well that Chance and his body and eyes and that triangle of skin she wanted to lick had been the source of four orgasms for her that week, even if he didn't know it), was off his game.

Okay, that wasn't fair.

Rob was as wonderful as always.

He just…only had eyes for Soph.

As it should be.

It was just…Chance was looking at her and she wanted him and…she couldn't have him (because complications). So, a barrier would be awesome right now.

"Um, Mist?"

She jumped again and nearly upended the platter *and* her plate this time. Tearing her eyes off Chance—a-fucking-gain, fucking hell—she glanced up at Carter, the oldest of the Jackson brothers. He had the same dark hair and olive coloring as Chance, but his eyes were a rich hazel. "Yeah?" she asked.

"Can I...have some?" he asked. "Or are you going to eat it all?"

Her stare dropped to her plate. Or more accurately, to the pile of salad that had engulfed her plate. "Shit," she muttered. "I'm sorry. I'm just..." *Lusting after your brother.*

Carter had a ready smile, just like the other Jacksons, and it came out then, as though he knew what was in her head. "No harm, no foul," he told her, snagging the platter, scooping some of the salad from her plate back on to it—bad manners or not—then passing it to Caleb (the Jacksons had a thing with C names), the middle brother, without taking any.

Before she could comment on that, he scooped up a healthy portion from her plate onto his then smiled again. "See? All good."

Out of nowhere, her eyes prickled.

God.

Why did she have to be such a crier?

But what he'd done was really sweet, and Rob aside, no one had done sweet for her in a long, long time.

"Thanks," she whispered.

His fingers came to her chin, brushed lightly over her jaw, studying her eyes (no doubt glassy), and smiling gently. "Anytime." He leaned in a bit, voice lowering. "I know us Jacksons can be a lot to take in." He straightened, smoothing back a lock of her hair that had gotten stuck on the stubble of his cheek. His grin made a reappearance. "But you'll get used to us."

Unbidden, her gaze slid from Carter to Chance, whose emerald eyes blazed with something she might think was jealously, if not for the fact that they didn't know each other, and she was sitting sandwiched between his brother and sister.

Carter shifted and she glanced at him, saw that he was looking at Chance, too, his lips turned up at the expression on his brother's face. "I think you'll be getting used to him, too," he murmured after a moment, turning in his chair so his hazel eyes locked on hers. There was something intense in them, as well. Not jealousy and not solely amusement, though that was there, also. This was attraction, firmly banked, not to be acted on.

Misty released a breath.

At least *this* Jackson had some fucking sanity.

"Though I don't think he even realizes how much."

"I'm not getting used to anyone—" she began, finding it difficult to keep her focus on Carter when she could feel Chance's gaze boring into her. Also, she only *began* because before she could finish the rest of her sentence, Chance called over the chatter of the table, "Rob?"

Her brother pulled himself out of his Sophie daze and turned to Chance. "Yeah?"

"You care if I date your sister?"

The table went silent, forks freezing in mid-air, the conversation dying out, many pairs of eyes darting from Chance to Misty to Rob. Waves crashed in the distance, seagulls cried, but for all intents and purposes, the world went quiet...at least their little slice of it.

Rob slowly set down his fork, face an unreadable mask. "You going to hurt her?"

Misty made a noise of disgust. "Neither of you gets a say in my love life—"

"You going to hurt *my* sister?" Chance countered.

"No," Rob said.

"Then there you have it," Chance told him. "I'm not going to hurt Misty, either."

That was really shitty male logic. So, if Rob hurt Soph, then Chance would hurt her? Or vice versa? Or was it because neither of them planned to hurt anyone? And anyway, shouldn't she be the one deciding all of this—or at least ending the conversation that pertained to her and her dating life that was being conducted as though she weren't in the room.

Sighing, she rubbed her forehead, a headache beginning to form.

Everyone else appeared to be stymied by the shitty male logic, because there was only more silence, minus the waves and gulls.

Well, she might not be able to cure her headache without some Tylenol, but she could damn sure cure this silence. "First," she began. "No one needs to ask permission to date me, like I'm some fucking heroine from a historical novel—shit, sorry, Mrs. Jackson—"

"Martha, please," Mrs. Jackson said. "No need for formalities."

"Right, um, sorry for cursing, Martha."

"I have five boys and a daughter, honey. I'm used to cursing, particularly around the dinner table."

"Oh." A beat. "Right."

She nodded, silently telling Misty to go on.

Right. Misty cleared her throat and powered through. "I'm an adult, and I can decide who I want"—she cut a glare at Chance—"or *don't want* to see."

More silence.

"Second?" Chance asked.

She blinked. "What?"

"You said 'first.'" His elbows plunked onto the table, and he leaned forward, and hell if it didn't feel like he was six inches from her rather than six feet. "That points to you having a second reason for turning me down the other day."

Quiet. Gulls. Waves.

Eyes on her, waiting for an answer.

And seriously, why in the fuck did he do this at the dinner table?

Probably, because he was smart enough to know it would be harder for her to turn him down in front of his family.

Sighing, she went back to rubbing her head. "Second, because it's too complicated."

"How?"

This question was from Soph, not Chance.

Relieved to tear her eyes from the man six feet that felt like six inches across from her, she turned to Soph, who for some fucking reason, was smiling. "If things go wrong, I could mess up this. You're happy. You guys are all happy. If Chance and I don't work out"—she glanced at Rob—"things could get uncomfortable, and you might not have *this*." She waved a hand at the table, which before then had been filled with laughter, teasing, and a multitude of conversations.

Rob was quiet for a long moment, long enough for her fucking stare to be drawn back to Chance. The man had goddamned tractor beams for eyes.

Then her brother spoke, and her gaze whipped back to his, knowing he would see it her way.

He'd lost too much not to.

"It's only a date, Dewdrop," he said and shifted so he could meet Chance's gaze.

"What?"

Rob didn't so much as look at her. "Take care of my sister."

"I—excuse me?" she began sputtering. "What the hell is wrong with—?"

But then someone began passing platters again, forks began moving to mouths, conversation resumed, seemingly no one perturbed by her continued sputtering and then her gaping like a fish.

Chance pushed back his chair, rounded the table, and bent down to murmur in her ear, "Tomorrow. Seven o'clock."

6

PIRATE'S BOOTY

Chance

"This is complete and utter bullshit," Misty snapped.

He bit back a grin when she slammed the pieces of the puzzle they were working on down onto the replica pirate's table and stalked away.

Maybe this wasn't the best idea.

But they'd been driving by on the way to the restaurant, and she'd off-handedly mentioned that she had seen this place a million times and had always wanted to try it.

Chance hadn't been able to resist flipping a U-turn, pulling into the parking lot, and seeing if they had availability.

Luckily they had…in the Pirate's Booty room.

Which sounded like some sort of twisted sex shop or orgy location but was really a small set of two rooms that had been successfully crafted into an escape room complete with buried treasure, a ship's wheel, plenty of pretend rum, and multiple puzzles that had both him and Misty struggling to solve them in the allotted one-hour time frame.

Truthfully, he hadn't been too focused.

Mostly because the moment he'd turned around and pulled

into the parking lot of Escape Rooms R Us, he'd been captivated by the pleasure on Misty's face.

Surprise that he'd drop everything he had planned to do something she wanted.

Joy when he'd taken her hand and led her inside, securing that spot in Pirate's Booty.

Excitement when they'd been led into the dark room and watched the video. She'd jumped at the fake thunder and lightning, allowing him to slip an arm around her waist and "comfort" her.

Now frustration because their time was running out and they had to solve this puzzle to win.

So, Misty was competitive in addition to caring about her brother and his sister and his family's future happiness. She was sweet enough to be surprised that he would go a little out of his way and change his plans to do something that would make her smile. Add in beautiful with a sexy body, enough spine to turn him down even though she was attracted to him, and soft enough to jump at fake lightning and thunder.

He liked her.

Enough that it might be a problem.

Because he preferred things light and casual, to be with a woman for as long as it worked for both of them. He preferred that fun, fucking, and then ending in friendship, and he was starting to think that he didn't *want* friendship with a woman like Misty.

She was…different.

She made him wonder if he could do different, too.

Except, he didn't play for keeps.

Not because he got off on hurting women. Not at all. He just didn't think the type of commitment his parents had found, what Soph had found, was worth the risk. His job was dangerous (though less so now that he'd left his work at the FBI and the DEA and had started his own investigation firm). But still, it might mean that he left a good woman alone, mourning him, and God, if he took it too far and made a family, he might leave his kids without a father.

He'd almost had that.

His dad had almost died.

He wouldn't do that to the people he cared about.

But…Misty made that decision, born of a boy's fear that the man who'd been all but a superhero would die, seem a little short-sighted.

What would it be like if he *did* play for keeps?

Because he'd spent only a couple of hours with her—most of them sitting across the table wanting to kill Carter for daring to lean close and talk to her, making her smile—and already letting her down gently was so fucking far off the map, it might as well be on another planet.

And then he was considering that he might very well get a spaceship to start mapping out the galaxy.

Fun. Fucking. Yes.

It was the friendship part he was reconsidering for the first time in his life.

"We only have two minutes left," Misty said, jarring him out of his thoughts, her cheeks flushed, her hair mussed from running her hands through it in frustration. Those tiger's eyes swirled with emotion in the dim light, feelings flitting through them so fast that he couldn't decipher them.

But then they settled on determination.

And that spaceship took flight.

Maybe the fun and fucking didn't have to end at friendship.

Maybe the risk of leaving something behind was minimal when compared to the risk of never going for it in the first place.

Fear down his spine.

But was it fear because he was considering breaking every rule because Misty was different from any woman he'd ever met before, or fear because he might not experience it at all?

That he wasn't sure of.

That he didn't have time to delve into any further.

Misty crossed back over to him, snatched his hand, dragged him to the table where they were supposed to be organizing the puzzle pieces on what he assumed was a built-in sensor.

Either that or the people behind the cameras in this room were watching very closely.

"We need to figure this out!"

He concentrated, for the first time in nearly an hour, not on the woman who smelled like hibiscus flowers and coconut and whose curves were distracting as hell in those tight jeans, but on the puzzle on the table in front of them. There was no doubt she'd been doing the heavy lifting of the puzzle-solving portion of events, and he supposed—with fifty-five seconds left on the clock—that he should begin pulling his weight, too.

A quick study of the letters.

T-Y-O-B-O

A glance at the paper she'd uncovered in the buried treasure. It had been written in code and said, "A pirate's favorite thing."

The five slots for those pieces—gold coins he realized now—sending an impressed thought into the universe for the people who'd come up with this room and their stick-to-it-ness to the theme.

Then he brushed Misty's fingers aside, rearranged the letters (B-O-O-T-Y), and placed them in the proper slots just as the clock wound down.

Three. Two. One...

He got the Y in.

The lights came on, and the far door swung open.

And Misty—once she was done gaping at the open door and the puzzle pieces—smiled wide, threw her arms up, and did a little dance, singing, "Pirate's Booty! Pirate's Booty! Pirate's—"

He kissed her.

It wasn't the first kiss he'd planned—that being later, on her front porch, soft and sweet and hopefully coaxing her into inviting him in for more kisses (and other things). Instead, it was hot and needy and had his cock hard faster than that spaceship rocketing through the air searching for reasons to keep her.

Forever.

Her chant was against his lips, on his tongue, and then her arms were around him...and then her *moan* was against his tongue, her fingers in his hair, and she was leaping into his arms so that he had the fucking glorious pleasure of having her ass in his hands as she laid a kiss on him that had him spinning and knocking the locks and keys and fake rum bottles and gold pieces from the pirate's table to the ground.

It was a kiss that would have had him stripping her down and getting some of *his* favorite thing—booty—if not for the throat clearing.

The *persistent* throat clearing.

Persistent and loud enough to let him know that it hadn't been the first time that throat clearing had happened.

Reluctantly, he released Misty's mouth, nearly forgetting about the throat clearing and taking it again when she made a soft mewling sound of protest, her lids half-closed, the tiger's eyes darkened to a rich amber.

He glanced up and over her shoulder, saw the kid who'd let them in here with bright pink cheeks. "Um," the teenager said, "you need to take your picture up front."

The soft—and embarrassed—words seemed to snap Misty back into herself.

He watched her cheeks grow pinker now, but then she straightened her shoulders, sighed, and brushed her mouth across his. "I want my victory picture."

"Okay," he murmured, willing his cock to soften.

"Chance?"

His brows lifted.

"To get my victory picture, you have to put me down." She pressed her lips to his jaw. "Or at least step back, so I can climb down."

He didn't want to do either.

His hands were still on her ass, her legs spread wide and wrapped around him.

But he stepped back and set her feet on the ground anyway. Then nearly groaned when she bent and started picking up gold coins and keys and fake rum bottles and locks.

That *ass*.

Fuck, any softening of his cock was done for.

To save himself the embarrassment of coming in his pants and the poor teenage boy whose cheeks had gone somehow even redder, Chance bent and helped her, even though he really wanted to continue enjoying the view. Instead, he made a mental note to fuck her that way so he could get a perfect view of that naked *booty* of hers and grabbed the last of the gold pieces before taking her hand and leading her from the room.

Trailing the kid into the lobby area.

Standing still while she sorted through the props and chose the ones she wanted—and the ones (yes, plural) she wanted him to hold. He took them when she extended them then promptly set them back into the basket.

"I—"

He slid an arm around Misty's waist, hauled her close. "Smile for the camera, baby."

The flash went.

And for the record, he thought it was the best victory photo ever.

SCARVES FOR EVERYONE

Misty

SHE HAD a picture in her purse of her in Chance's arms, his head close to hers, whispering in her ear, while she grinned at the camera.

Smiling like she was having the time of her life.

And she kind of was.

Escape room. Check.

Escape room *conquered*. Also, check.

A kiss to end all kisses, followed by a warm, sexy man nuzzling her neck and telling her to smile. Another checkmark.

Then holding her hand to the car, driving her to her favorite restaurant (whether that was by chance since it was the only Italian place in town, or if Rob and Soph had dished, she didn't know), and taking her hand again as they'd walked into Tony's, while they waited for their table, which took a while because they'd missed their reservation due to the escape room diversion, and until he'd deposited her into her seat.

Perfect date.

All her worrying about complications was for nothing.

Chance was *awesome*.

He was funny and charming, telling her stories about his job as a private investigator, which she thought sounded really freaking cool. But he told her it was less stakeout and more scouring through copious amounts of online records, requesting and rereading old police or government files, and the occasional bit of fieldwork, depending on if he'd been hired by an agency or by a private citizen. Of course, he'd said that occasional bit of fieldwork mostly involved interviews, though it had a dash of staking out, along with the occasional taking down and handcuffing of bad guys until the authorities got there.

The last two were both cool and a little scary.

"Really," he said when she told him that. "People think it's a lot more exciting than it is. Though I can't lie and say it's not occasionally dangerous. I just try to be smart and safe, because I have plans to continue seeing a gorgeous blonde who likes all things booty."

She snorted and shook her head, glancing down at her menu and pretending to study it even though she ordered the same thing every time. She thought he was underselling himself significantly, but she kind of dug that he wasn't super cocky. Confident, yes, but not over the top. It was sexy, that confidence, enough that she wanted to scoot her chair around the table and sit next to him.

Okay, not sit.

She wanted to crawl into his lap and kiss him again.

But she could control herself (barely), and, anyway, she had other questions. "You didn't want to work for the FBI like your dad?"

"I did work for them. For a time," he said, surprising her.

Her brows lifted in question.

He answered without her saying it aloud. "It was my dream for a long time, to do what my dad did, and for a while it was awesome."

His eyes held a glint of pain, and she reached across the table for his hand. "What happened?"

Misty hadn't expected him to answer, let alone to give her the truth, straight up without any varnish. "Lost a couple people I cared about because of shitty orders and fucking stupid regulations. The shit that was supposed to keep them safe sent them into a mission with their wrists handcuffed behind their backs and their feet shackled. I decided I wasn't going into anymore situations that I couldn't handle my way and that I wasn't going to let the fucking rules get in the way of someone's safety."

She inhaled sharply. "I'm sorry."

A nod, his hand turning over in hers, weaving their fingers together, his eyes losing that glint of pain. "Thanks, honey. It was a long time ago, but thank you, all the same." He brushed his thumb over her wrist. "Not to be an asshole, but I don't really like to talk about this shit."

"I'm sorry," she said again.

"Nothing to apologize for." He squeezed her hand. "I try to live my life by being honest, giving answers to genuine questions when someone asks."

Her brows lifted, but he kept talking.

"It's easier that way, means that the shit doesn't get heavy and eat at me, eat at whatever I'm building with the pretty woman sitting across the table from me."

Her cheeks heated. "You don't have much of a filter, do you?"

He grinned. "No. Never have. Not gonna start now."

Maybe that should be a problem. He didn't seem like the kind of guy who sugarcoated things, and she didn't exactly have the thickest skin, so she might get hurt. But he also didn't seem mean, and she'd grown up with Rob, who was also a straight-shooter. Plus, he'd brought her to the escape room and held her hand, and now they were sitting across the table at Tony's, her favorite place ever.

But her mind was drifting because Soph had told her a little of what Chance's dad had done to get her away from her family (thus leading to his adopting her all those years ago), and she wondered about the *occasionally dangerous* part of his job. But then again, Chance said he was out of the FBI and on his own now.

Did that make it better or worse?

She didn't know, but she supposed the reality was that a lot of jobs were dangerous, and it sounded like he was doing good, important work that was awesome.

Just like Chance.

A leg brushing hers under the table had her glancing up, almost gasping at the intensity in his eyes.

"Is it too much for you?"

Her breath caught.

Serious.

He'd suddenly gone so, *so* serious.

And she had the feeling that if she answered wrong, he'd walk her to her door after dinner, kiss her on the cheek, and then they would never go on another date again. It would be family dinners and friendship and nothing romantic.

One date. They'd had one date, and that was such a painful thought it had her lungs burning, her heart aching, her throat going tight.

So…it was key that she answered this correctly.

"It's not too much for me."

He opened his mouth like he was going to say something, the intensity in his gaze not abating in the least.

So, she went on before he could. "I was thinking that you are doing important work, and that while it might be occasionally dangerous, a lot of jobs can be dangerous. Hell, I could trip at the shop and impale myself on a basket of knitting needles tomorrow. And then I was thinking that what you're doing is awesome in a way that's cool because I've seen a lot of action movies and I can pretend that you're like a hero in one of those, even though I know that isn't reality, but it's cool anyway because you're modest about it." His eyes gentled. She kept talking. "And finally, I was thinking that if you're a guy who can be modest about something like a job that's *occasionally dangerous* then you're pretty awesome, and I'm guessing your job is, too, and that a woman who was with you would be lucky to be with such an awesome guy."

"You think I'm awesome?"

He *really* didn't have much of a filter.

Well, she could do the same.

"Yes."

"You think my job is awesome?"

"You're helping people." She shrugged. "I don't see how anyone couldn't see it was awesome and worth whatever kind of risk *occasionally dangerous* might bring you."

A ripple went through him. His eyes went intense again, but there wasn't the sense that he was going to be leaving her on the porch with a kiss on the cheek. This was an intensity that said he'd be in her bed…and wouldn't be leaving.

And just when her breath was catching at that very pleasurable thought—based on that kiss in the Pirate's Booty Room—the heat faded, dropped down to a simmer.

He grinned, mischief in his eyes. "Impale yourself on knitting needles?"

Another shrug. "It's possible."

His fingers found hers. "For the record, I'm not a superhero, babe."

"I get that, but I still think you might be a normal hero," she said, knowing that she should probably say something more, but their entrees arrived, and they pulled their hands apart, spending the next couple of minutes sorting out plates and refills of their wine and utensils and first bites.

Hers: fettuccini alfredo with extra mushrooms, no chicken.

His: spaghetti bolognese with two of Tony's special meatballs.

Then she'd chewed and swallowed and started to scoop up another bite when he asked, "Why yarn?"

She set down her fork. Apparently, they were done discussing occasionally dangerous. "Why my store?"

A nod. "Or more accurately, how did you come to open your own yarn store?"

"It's a boring story," she warned, "but since I have a lot of practice at telling it"—people asked her a lot at the shop—"I'll give you the Cliff's Notes version. My mom was a knitter, taught me and my brother—"

"Rob?"

Misty grinned. "Yup. Rob is as good as me, maybe better at some of the stitches." She giggled at the expression on Chance's face. "We used to knit every night with my mom. It was like our...decompressing time. We'd tell her about our day and whatever was big or important during that point in our lives. We'd talk and eat cookies she'd baked and just...be together. My dad was there, too, usually watching some game, while Rob and I talked her ear off as she put us to work on whatever project she was working on."

His hand found hers and squeezed again. "That sounds nice."

"It was." A wave of sadness washed over her at the memories, but it was a long time ago. She had lots of practice at hiding it away. "The shop was actually her dream," she said, telling Chance something no one else knew except for Rob, Mags, and Frankie. "Mom was saving up for it, had plans for classes and projects to put up in the windows. Then when my parents passed and I was spending the evenings on my couch, knitting by myself, I got it in my head to give her that, even if she wasn't here, to give *me* that, the connection, the dream." She put her fork in her pasta and swirled it around. "It became my dream, and I've loved it from the first moment I opened Tangled, even if I didn't come up with the idea myself."

"Mist." His voice was gentle, and her eyes stung.

Her gaze drifted up to his. "Yeah?"

"I think she'd be really proud."

The breath froze in her lungs because he sounded genuine, because his eyes told her he *was* genuine. And suddenly the emotion, the sadness, it wasn't so deep. It was on the surface, and she was feeling vulnerable.

Which the man seemed to understand.

Because he was already reaching across the table when a tear slid out of the corner of her eye, and without missing a beat, he wiped it away then pointed at her plate. "Eat up, honey," he said, "and then tell me if you think my entire family is going to get hand-knitted scarves for Christmas this year, courtesy of Soph."

She laughed, and yes, it sounded a little watery, but it was laughter and enough to snap her out of the sad.

Enough that she said, "Oh yeah," and relished in *his* laughter.

Enough that she then changed the subject to lighter topics and enjoyed even more laughter as they ate their pasta and had tiramisu for dessert and lingered over espressos.

Enough so that when he walked her up onto her front porch, she didn't hesitate to invite him inside.

Not for a nightcap.

For her.

Thankfully, he took her up on that.

8

ON TOP

Chance

SHE WAITED for him to open the car door when he asked her to, didn't hesitate when he took her hand as they walked up to her porch.

It felt right to wrap those delicate fingers in his.

So fucking right.

Almost as much as everything she'd given him.

You're pretty awesome, and I'm guessing your job is too.

Acceptance. Humor. And him reconsidering what had made him keep his distance from women all these years. Misty was different from all the other women, seeing him in a way that made him want to take the risk of loving her, of bringing the risk of *him* into her life, mostly because she thought his job was important and awesome and even though he'd been straight with her about the occasional danger, she hadn't balked.

At all.

Plus, he'd never had someone lay out their feelings for him quite in that way before. As straight as him, from a woman who felt so deep that she'd shed a tear over bread and drinks and the memory of her parents.

Which made him want to pull her close and never let her go. Like *never*.

Even though he told himself that he wouldn't get in this deep with a woman, now he was thinking that when it was the *right* woman, a man didn't have a choice to *not* get in deep.

To jump in knowing it might bring the best adventure of his life.

Because he'd fallen for her.

Over an auto accident, through a family dinner and a trip to her yarn store. Over pirate's booty and victory photos. But most especially over Italian food because they'd chatted through dinner, moving on to lighter topics rather than the heavy shit they'd begun their meal with. He now knew she liked to walk on the beach in the early morning but hated all other types of exercise, even though her brother occasionally forced her to go hiking with him and Soph. He knew her favorite color was purple, her favorite food was the fettuccini Alfredo from Tony's with extra mushrooms, that she couldn't resist chocolate, and that she preferred beer to wine.

He'd told her more about his job, about his time in the FBI, though he'd kept it lighter with funny stories of agents and their cases after he'd finished with his laying it all out. Then she'd gotten his favorite movie—*Die Hard*—out of him, along with his favorite meal—his mom's chicken pot pie and home-made biscuits—favorite beer—anything IPA—and the favorite place he'd visited—Iceland.

Which meant he also got the same answers out of her (*The Princess Bride*, the aforementioned fettuccini, Corona with lime, and Vermont during the fall).

He liked her.

She was funny.

She was cute as hell.

She was…a lot. So much so, he was reconsidering his plan to coax his way into her house because she meant more than trying to get into her pants and have fun for a night with limited strings attached and both of them scratching an itch.

She was more than fun, fucking, and friends.

He wanted more than that.

Which was...terrifying, and also kind of liberating? That he didn't have to keep being afraid of something that might happen. Instead, it was happening and it was great and he wasn't a stupid man, so he could understand this wasn't an opportunity to pass up.

Even if that meant he wouldn't get laid tonight.

Slow and steady and...permanent.

Oh fuck, he wanted permanent.

Misty reached into her purse and came up with her keys, unlocking the door and pushing it open before she faced him and leaned back against the jamb. "Do you want to come in?"

His heart still pounding from his realization, he told her softly, "I shouldn't."

Her brows lifted and a flash of hurt trailed across her eyes, but she nodded, started to step back, and he found himself telling the truth.

"If I do, I'll want another one of those kisses," he murmured, "and then I don't think it'll stop with just kissing." He tucked a strand of her hair behind her ear. "It'll end up with you naked beneath me and—"

"Good."

Chance blinked. "What?"

"I want to be naked and beneath you, though I'd prefer to be naked and on top of you because it's easier for me to come that way, and I like orgasms. If it's missionary, I really have to work for it. Which is fine, and based on that kiss earlier, I probably wouldn't have to work *too* hard for it. It's just that I like my breasts being touched and my nipples"—a swathe of pink on her cheeks, and seriously, *that* was the part that made her blush? —"sucked, and that's...um...easier when I'm on top." She cleared her throat, straightened her shoulders, and met his eyes.

"Truth is, I've had enough orgasms courtesy of my vibrator, so I'd like one courtesy of you."

Silent.

He was silent for way too long, processing what she'd just said.

Long enough that her tiger's eyes flickered with pain again. Long enough that he still couldn't come up with anything to say.

No witty comeback. No explanation that they should take this slow since it was important. No romantic words.

He had...*nothing*.

The only thing he knew was that he didn't want the hurt to be present in her eyes or mind or heart, and that he certainly didn't want it to be courtesy of him. And maybe it simply boiled down to him wanting her more than he'd wanted any other woman.

Wanting more *with* her.

He grabbed her purse from her hands, dropped it on the floor inside the hall, and nudged her back, slamming the door closed behind him and flicking the lock. Her lips parted, and that was as much encouragement as he needed.

He kissed her.

Her tongue hit his mouth, her fingers drove into his hair, and she jumped, her legs coming around his waist.

Groaning, he walked her back until he found the first horizontal surface—a hall table—and propped her on top of it, breaking the kiss so he could trail his mouth along her jaw, lave her earlobe, nip at her throat, use his nose to nudge the straps down on the sexy dress she was wearing.

Then nudged it further.

Because she'd been pretty damned clear about liking her breasts touched, and he couldn't fucking wait to get his mouth on her nipples.

He tugged the bodice down, revealing midnight blue lace and gorgeous breasts.

"Chance," she breathed when he bent enough to suck one hard nipple through the fabric of her bra. Her fingers tightened, and he didn't delay, just tugged the material to the side, sucked her nipple deep, and soaked in the gloriousness of her arching against him, his name on her tongue again, her legs clenching around him.

He sucked the pink tip until it turned rosy, until she was panting and moaning. Then he kissed his way over to her other breast, repeated the motions with her other nipple. She was shuddering beneath him, her whole body quivering.

"Chance," she moaned.

"Mmm?"

"Kiss me." An order.

One he didn't heed until he'd kissed her breasts for good measure, kissed his way back up her throat. Only then did he take her mouth again.

But he didn't just take her mouth. He slid his hands over her body, hiked up her skirt, trailed his fingers along her thighs until he reached her pussy. The lace covering it was absolutely drenched through.

"Fuck, baby," he groaned.

"Inside," she demanded. "Please, Chance. I need you inside."

He slid a finger beneath the waistband of her panties, sliding the material to the side, and tracing through the wet folds. Drenched. Absolutely fucking drenched.

She reached for the button of his slacks, flicked it open.

But he was already dropping to his knees, his cock hard and aching beneath the zipper she luckily hadn't been able to tug down. He spread her thighs and leaned in, needing to taste her. Fuck, she smelled incredible, and he could see her pussy, swollen, pink, and glistening.

She tasted better.

Misty gasped and gripped his head tight, holding his mouth to her, hips bucking as she ground herself against him. His tongue worked her, dipping in and dragging up, circling her clit, flicking it rapidly, sucking it when it swelled, and then giving her the barest graze of teeth.

She jerked.

His name on her tongue cracked.

Those fingers held on to his hair to an almost painful degree.

Then she fractured, her head falling back against the wall, her thighs clenching on his shoulders, and she came against his tongue.

Fuck, she was pretty.

Her skin flushed, sweat glistening on her collarbones. He brought her down slowly, and then straightened, licked that salty sheen off her skin, nibbled at her slender throat before finding her lips again. The kiss was lazy and slow, teasing and warm. Until it wasn't.

Until it was hot and hard, their tongues dueling, their breaths intermingling, their hands frenzied.

She gave him everything in that kiss.

And then she reached down and tugged the zipper of his pants down, reached in and freed him, her delicate fingers wrapping around him and stroking him from base to head. His hips pulsed forward, wanting more, but fine with not getting it.

At least until she shifted on that table and her wet pussy grazed his cock.

"Wait, baby," he said.

"I'm on birth control," she whispered, shifting closer. "And clean."

He'd never had sex without a condom.

But he had been tested recently. "I'm clean, too."

"Good." And then she shifted forward again, taking him inside. He would have had to be dead to resist her, and for the record, he wasn't dead in the least. He felt alive for the first time since his partner and his best friend had died on that mission, since he'd worried himself into a terrible spiral after his dad had nearly died. Since he'd decided the *only* way to live was to keep himself separate and safe.

Suddenly, he understood why Soph, who'd been through so much, had risked everything to be with Rob, why his mom had never stopped his dad from returning to work, despite the danger.

Because he felt alive with Misty in a way he'd never dreamed was possible.

And it changed *everything*.

His hips shot forward, burying himself deep, hands going to her waist, angling her so she could better take him in.

"Oh, my God," she whispered. "That's so fucking good."

And it was.

It was better than good. He'd never felt anything better in his entire life. She was hot and tight, wet and holding him to her, meeting him stroke for stroke, hips bucking, fingers sliding up his chest to grip his shoulders, nails digging in.

He swept her up into his arms, took a step to the left, and pinned her against the wall, thrusting deep and hard, bending his head to suck her nipples again, hands gripping her ass. Too tight. Probably, too fucking tight, but he couldn't find the strength to loosen it, not when she was so fucking perfect around him, not when she was moaning and moving against him, not when...she was exploding, coming on his cock, pussy clenching, moisture drenching him, the convulsions sending him over the edge on a rough groan.

She stilled and went limp, arms and legs tight against him.

They were both breathing heavily, his pants were around his thighs, her dress was bunched around her waist.

He summoned enough energy to pull out, yank up his pants so he didn't trip, and then brought Misty close, cuddling her against his chest. She blinked up at him, her eyes satisfied and drowsy, her lips swollen from their kisses. Beautiful. So fucking beautiful.

More so by the way she rested her head against his chest

and sighed, her soft words laced with humor reaching his ears. "I guess wall sex is almost as good as me being on top."

He glanced down. "Almost?"

A nod. A smile that was wicked tempered by sweet. A glance that stole his breath.

Because this woman was so different from any other he'd met.

Because he fucking *liked* her.

Especially, when her hand came to his jaw.

"Unless you want to carry me to my bedroom and prove me wrong?"

"Is that a challenge or a request?" he asked, turning and starting down the hall. There were only three doors in this cottage. It wouldn't be hard to find the bedroom.

First door, bathroom.

Second door, closet.

"Either," Misty said, her fingers working on the buttons of his shirt. "Both."

Third door, bedroom.

He moved inside, dropped her on the bed, and followed her down, bringing his mouth very close to hers.

"Accepted," he said against her lips.

"The challenge or the request?"

A nip of that bottom lip. "Either." A beat. "Both."

She grinned.

And he just had to kiss that smile off her mouth...then he had to kiss her other places because of the challenge.

And the request.

9

COMPLICATIONS

Misty

SHE ROLLED OVER, deliciously sore, and expected to encounter a warm male next to her in bed.

They'd had sex three times.

She'd gotten her quota of orgasms courtesy of something other than her hand or her vibrators. It had been glorious...but now her hand was encountering cool sheets.

Frowning, she sat up, saw the pillow next to her was dented, the blankets had been tucked up and over her, and the other side of the bed was empty.

Huh.

Maybe he was in the bathroom?

She waited a few minutes, listening for the pipes, the sound of footsteps, water rushing in her gorgeous pedestal sink.

But her house was silent.

And she felt her brows draw together further.

Then he must have gone out for coffee and cinnamon rolls and was going to bring her back some much needed sustenance. That was what the man from the date last night would do, the sweet, thoughtful man who'd held her hand, taken her to her favorite restaurant, the escape room, and kissed her like she mattered then made love to her until they'd both collapsed into sleep.

So, she would snuggle down in her blankets, her awesome mattress, and wait for him to get back.

Letting her eyes slide closed, she burrowed in, allowed herself to go drowsy, and then settled in to wait.

Then settled in some more.

Then some more.

Then...she reached for her phone, checked the time, and realized it was nearly ten, nearly time for her to open the shop, something she normally didn't have to do on Sundays, but something she had to do today because she had a private class to teach, and that meant she had to hurry up and get ready. Which meant she couldn't snuggle under the covers and wait for Chance.

Maybe he'd had a break in one of the cases he was talking about last night and had needed to get to work. Maybe that work had been early, and he hadn't wanted to wake her.

Maybe...he'd left her a note.

Yes, he definitely would have left her a note.

She tossed back the covers, glanced toward one nightstand and then the other. No note.

Right.

Maybe it was in the kitchen. If it was her leaving a note, she would put it by the coffee pot, or in the bathroom, or... she began listing all the different locations in her mind where he might have left a note explaining that he had a break-through on a case that involved some mysterious private investigator stuff that he couldn't talk about or else he'd have to kill her.

She continued mentally listing locations through brushing her teeth and slapping on a quick face of makeup.

(And not finding a note in the bathroom).

She did more listing as she rifled through her closet and

yanked on a knitted sweater (she had to model her own wares), jeans, and comfortable boots.

(A note didn't mysteriously appear in her bedroom when she did this).

She did even *more* listing through pouring coffee into a travel mug and grabbing a granola bar from the basket she kept on the counter for just such rushed mornings.

(No note by the coffee pot. Neither by nor *in* the basket).

She did still more listing on the way to her garage, looking at the windshield of her car, the passenger's seat, the cup holder.

(No notes).

Then she did her final listing when she walked into Tangled: Yarn Emporium and checked the front door and the mail slot.

(There weren't any notes there either).

But still, she was hopeful.

Because maybe he'd gotten called out quickly, and hadn't had time to leave a note, and he didn't have her number— except he *did* have her number. She'd given it to him after the accident. So maybe he hadn't had a chance to call or leave that note, and he would call later.

Like during lunch.

(He didn't).

Or after she closed.

(He didn't).

Or maybe the next day.

(He didn't).

The next *week*?

(He didn't).

And that was when the ball of dread that had been threatening to gather in her stomach coalesced into a giant, writhing, uncomfortable sphere of disappointment...and she couldn't lie, but that sphere also really hurt.

Because she'd thought they'd had a great night.

Because she'd thought they'd shared something.

And he was gone.

No word. No note. No call.

Not even a text.

She let go of her denial (and one might say the last bit of hope she'd held that this was all some emergency, strange misunderstanding and that Chance would come strolling through the shop's doors, apology on his lips) during her Saturday morning class.

Because Soph attended, ready to make herself an adorable cowl-necked sweater.

And in doing that, she asked Misty how the date had gone.

Misty had answered honestly—fantastic.

It was the rest of it that had gone bad.

Soph had gleefully clapped her hands together and asked when they were going out again. Then had promptly stopped and said, saving Misty from having to come up with an answer, "Oh, I forgot. He's on a job. Called and told me about it. So, it'll be a while then."

He'd talked to Soph?

He'd called *Soph* and not her? Not the woman he'd fucked into the wee hours of the night, making her think that she was special and meant something and—

Hurt wove its way through her, smothering the final embers of hope she'd (obviously now stupidly) held on to. "I—"

Mrs. Hutchinson pushed in through the door, the ringing of the bell drowned out by her shouting (because she only ever shouted), "I have a yarn emergency and I need you, Misty!" Then she began barreling through the store, her wide hips nearly knocking over displays that Misty had spent hours (hours!) organizing.

"We'll talk later," Soph had whispered out of the corner of her mouth, suitably scared of Mrs. Hutchinson, her yell-talking, her dangerous hips, and her perpetually annoyed attitude.

Mist felt the same.

Unfortunately, Mrs. Hutchinson had been a big part of the reason she'd made rent for the first years she'd been in business.

And had bought her house.

And paid off her car.

"Right," Misty said to Soph, not committing to the later talk.

Because Chance had held her hand and kissed her like she mattered and then left her after he'd slept with her.

No note. No text. No call.

This was why she hadn't wanted to go out with him.

Because she was a dumbass romantic and when people were nice to her, she melted, and when men held her hand and kissed her like she meant something and took her to escape rooms, she began to think of romantic things.

Like a second fantastic date.

Like *more* dates than two.

Like a future where she and Soph might become sisters-in-law in more ways than one.

Like a future with a man who held her hand and solved escape rooms with two seconds left by solving a puzzle to form the word "booty."

Complications.

Too fucking many of them.

No call. No text. No note.

God, that hurt. Even more that she'd opened her body to him—and her heart—and he hadn't even been able to bear staying the night.

Bear waking up next to her.

Her eyes stung. Her throat burned.

But luckily, Mrs. Hutchinson was in the midst of a yarn emergency and that quickly cured her stinging eyes and burning throat, especially since she had to crawl through her storeroom and unearth several boxes of very expensive yarn with slender strands of silver in them—Mrs. Hutchinson bought a dozen skeins—and by the time she washed the dust off her hands, it was time to teach.

Then, after class, several of her students had questions or comments or just wanted to shoot the shit about Stoneybrook—the storm that had knocked over the flag pole downtown, the announcement that Finn Stoneman was going to film his latest movie in town (mostly so he could stay close to his wife, Shannon, and kiddos), the news that Bob's Burgers had been sold and was going to become a sushi restaurant (a first for their small town, but one that Misty was wholeheartedly behind).

Which meant that Soph disappeared with a kiss on Misty's cheek, saying she would see her in two weeks, as she and Rob were going on a much-deserved vacation, leaving the following morning.

Saved by a trip to a private island.

Or rather, her brother and his wife's trip to that private island.

Either way, she knew as she closed up shop and headed home, that trip was going to give her two weeks to put Chance behind her.

To close off the romance, to drown the hope.

To categorize the date as a fun one-night stand rather than what she'd thought was the beginning of something.

To be able to lock everything down enough to pretend that she and Chance could be friendly acquaintances (not friends because friends didn't fuck and leave friends without a note or call or text, and she wasn't hopeful or romantic enough to let that slide, nor was she pathetic enough to sign up for a repeat of that same treatment).

Complications. These were the complications she'd hoped to avoid.

Because feeling like shit wasn't conducive for happy family gatherings.

Fucking hell.

Enough.

She would lock it down, would use these two weeks to convince herself that she and Chance had no chemistry, and that way she would be able to convince Rob and Soph that friendly acquaintances were all she and Chance would ever be.

And if it killed something inside her to do that, then so be it.

Life was full of disappointment.

She had Rob and Soph, her friends.

That was enough.

Because she sure as shit didn't need a man in her life who thought she wasn't worth that call or text or even a fucking note by a coffee pot.

10

WICKER

Chance

HE WHISTLED as he strolled up the sidewalk.

Two weeks since he'd seen her, and damn, but he was itching to taste and hold and laugh with Misty Hansen.

He'd gotten that one night, and it wasn't nearly enough.

Strolling down the little street, its cobblestones mismatched and slightly uneven, Chance knew he was a long way from Atlanta.

And he liked it.

Liked the quiet and safe neighborhoods, the way people waved to each other and said hello and seemed to know everything about each other.

He didn't miss the traffic, or the smog in the air, or the humidity of the big city.

Plus, he really liked the ocean air, the way the sky went orange and red and navy when the sun set.

But more than that, he seriously liked the blonde beauty who owned Tangled: Yarn Emporium.

His hand wrapped around the stainless steel handle, his mouth turning up into a smile before he was even through the door. Because Misty was standing at a display of yarn on the far end of the store, a basket in her arms as she reached up and shoved rolls of yarn onto the shelves.

The bell jingled and she said without looking over her shoulder, "I'll be right with you."

She rose on tiptoe, putting another paper-wrapped ball of yarn onto a shelf above her head, barely able to reach, and he made his way to her, coming up behind her and nudging it back so it wouldn't fall.

"I've got it, Cloudless."

Because that was what she was.

The cloudless sky, no hint of storm on the horizon. Beautiful and clear.

Misty jumped, going ramrod stiff, the basket falling to the ground, yarn balls skittering in all directions. Then she spun.

He thought she was going to throw her arms around him, to press those luscious breasts against his chest, to kiss him like she had that night—like he was water, and she was desperate to slake her thirst, but only with him.

Instead, she jabbed a finger into his chest, hard enough that he rocked back on his heels. "You have *got* to be kidding me."

Chance blinked. "What's up, baby?" he asked.

"What's. Up?" Her other hand lifted, shoved him back a step. "*What's up?*"

Okay, he didn't consider himself the smartest man around, but he knew he wasn't fucking stupid. He'd left Misty with a sleepy smile on her face, her limbs lax from pleasure, after getting a full night of her cute and sweet, and had gone to work for two weeks, and somehow during the last two weeks something had pissed her way the hell off.

He snagged her wrists, drew her close, inhaling that floral scent as he stared into her eyes.

They were swirling orbs of gold and brown and black, fury sending them sparking.

"What happened, baby?" he asked, genuinely concerned now. "Is everything okay?"

She plunked her hands on her hips. "You seriously *cannot* be this fucking stupid."

"What. Happened?" he repeated.

Her head dropped back; her sigh ripped through the air of the shop. "You are," she muttered, lifting her head, before bending and reaching for the scattered yarn. "You are seriously that stupid. Despite solving booty. Despite the charm at dinner. You are a fucking moron."

Okay, *now* he was getting pissed.

He inhaled, his exhale a hiss.

But he held on to his temper by a hairsbreadth.

"I had a great time with you, Cloudless," he gritted, going for calm. "I told you that night I wanted to see you again."

Her cheeks flared with color. "Yeah, you did," she snapped. "And then you disappeared off the planet for two weeks without one word or action to back that up. *I'm* not stupid. *I* know how to read signals when they're given to me."

He stepped into her, fury licking up his spine. "I was on a mission. I couldn't call because I was off the grid."

She stepped into *him*. "But you took the time to call Soph and let her know you were working?" she asked, her voice icy cold. "And you couldn't spare me ten seconds to write a note or call or text? *I* couldn't reach out to you. *I* don't have *your* number. And even if I did, it seems that wouldn't matter because you were still off-grid, and I'm guessing you wouldn't have had time for a chat."

"My work is important," he gritted out. "You said so yourself." They'd talked about his job. She knew it was complicated and delicate at times. She'd called it awesome.

Said he was a hero.

And he'd explained that it took him away from home often.

"I know it's important." Her lips pressed flat. "I don't believe I said it wasn't. But you left, Chance. Without a second thought, without a word, and I don't need someone who doesn't think *I'm* important."

"I don't think that," he said, cupping her cheek, holding it a little tighter when she would have yanked away. "And I didn't call Soph while I was on the mission. I talked to her before our date."

She froze. "Oh."

They stared at each other silently, the fury in her eyes having extinguished. But the hurt was still there, and her words proved to him how deep it ran, washed away his temper. "I waited," she whispered. "That morning, after the best fucking date of my life, after me thinking that it was the start of something that might end with me related to Soph in more ways than one—"

His head jerked.

She sighed, eyes sliding closed.

And continued speaking. "That morning, I snuggled down in bed and thought that the man who'd upended our dinner plans so I could solve the Mystery of the Pirate's Booty was going to walk right through the door of my bedroom with coffee and a cinnamon roll in his hand. Then I walked through my house thinking that surely you must have left me a note— on my pillow, my bathroom counter, by the coffee pot, or maybe in my granola bar basket."

She had a granola bar basket?

His lips twitched at her cute.

He supposed that it went along with the baskets on her nightstand, the ones on her island, the copious amount of wicker containers in this shop.

His woman had an addiction to baskets.

Well, there were worse addictions to have.

At least baskets were cheap.

And no, he wasn't worrying about the fact that he'd just thought of Misty as his woman. He'd be more worried if he hadn't. Because he hadn't been able to stop thinking about her since the moment she'd crashed into his SUV, and certainly not over these last two weeks.

She'd burrowed into him, and he'd decided to let her stay there.

But she was still talking, and what she said took away any amusement he'd held about copious amounts of wicker.

"Then I waited for you to come to the shop and ask me to lunch," she whispered, her eyes glimmering with tears. "*Then* I waited for you to call or text. For an entire week, I was hopeful but feeling that hope slowly chip away, getting tangled with disappointment and despair and…hating myself because I couldn't help but think that you didn't call because you didn't feel the same way about me and the date."

His gut twisted.

Fuck.

He hadn't thought.

He hadn't *even* thought that she might take it that way. Not when he'd mentioned the job.

Hadn't he? He certainly had told her that he might be away for a while, that he was leaving in the morning to chase down a lead. Chance scoured through his memories, *sure* he had, but as he kept going through that night, he couldn't actually recall telling her that he was leaving for a job.

They'd talked about a lot of things.

His schedule for the previous two weeks? That he would be out of contact the entire time?

That he wasn't sure of.

Fuck.

Her chin came up, those eyes still sparkling with tears, some escaping and clinging to her eyelashes. "I like myself," she said, voice growing hard as she dashed them away. "I'm fun and nice and a cool chick to hang out with. I like sports…well, I like hockey and not because it's something I'm supposed to pretend to enjoy. I watch it and yell at the players when they fuck up, and that's because I like it and I'm a cool chick and I'm freaking *fun* to spend time with!"

He reached for her.

She dodged, snagging a ball of yarn and throwing it at him.

"Mist—"

"So, regardless of the stupid as shit agreement you made with my brother to not hurt me—which you fucking failed at, by the way, because I'm not going to lie, you hurt me, and you hurt me deep—"

Fuck.

She pelted him with another ball of yarn.

"I," she went on, launching more yarn at him, causing it to bean off his face, his chest, his stomach, "*really* don't like feeling like garbage. So, fuck off, Chance. Just go away, and we'll be simple acquaintances and keep all the complications that come out of this shit going south far, far away from our siblings' lives."

He snagged her wrist. "Misty, I fucked up."

Her eyes flared. "Yes, you did." She tried to tug her hand free.

"Misty, baby, I'm sorry," he said. "I fucked up. I'm—"

"You said that already." She tugged at her hand. He held tight. "Let me go."

"No, honey, not until you understand."

"Let. Me. *Go.*"

"Not until I've said what I'm going to say."

She kept tugging. He leaned closer, pressing her back against the yarn. "Let. Me—"

He placed one finger over her mouth.

She bit him.

Hard.

Cursing, he yanked his hand back. "Cloudless," he muttered.

"I don't even know what that means," she snapped.

Now was not the time to explain the name to her. He could

tell her later, after they'd figured this out. Because if this moment had proved anything to him, it was that the thought of letting her go was fucking *agony*. He'd do anything to keep her in his life, even just barely knowing her. "Please, stop fighting against me and listen."

"I will *not* stop fighting you, Chance *Fucking* Jackson. I will not *listen* to you. You're scum. A scummy scum…bag who has sex with women, leaves them heartbroken, and then thinks he can return to jump into bed with them again," she snapped. "Well, I might get used once, but I'm not going to get used twice."

She was furious at him, and he knew why.

He'd fucked up, hadn't told her he was leaving, hadn't woken her up to tell her he was going. They'd shared something he'd known was special, that she'd thought was special, too, and he'd left her hanging in the wind, twisting in the breeze, spending the last two weeks distorting everything that had happened between them.

He'd hurt her.

His only hope of fixing things between them was to lay the truth on her.

"I thought the same, sweetheart."

Her hand had snatched another ball of yarn from one of the baskets, was clutching it tightly, her arm ratcheted back.

"I thought the same," he said, stepping closer, moving directly into the line of fire. "I woke up that morning, not psyched to go to work for the first time but fucking anxious to get it over with so I could get back to you. I like you, Misty. A lot more than I should probably, considering that we've had one date and you totaled my car."

Her cheeks went pink.

"I should have left a note or woken you up," he said, cupping her cheek, moving slowly so as not to startle her. "But I swear, I thought that I'd told you I was going to be away for a couple of weeks. I—" He inhaled, released it slowly. "I wouldn't do that," he said. "If you knew how I grew up, you would know I would never do that."

She softened in his hold, her eyes gentling. "What happened when you were growing up?"

He wove his fingers into her hair, feeling the silk drift over his skin, and gave it to her. Because it was the only way. "You know a little of what my dad did with the FBI and a couple of other organizations he can't talk about, but I don't know if you knew he worked *deep* undercover. He'd be gone for months, and we didn't know when he would make it home."

Sympathy softened the lines of her face. "That must have been hard."

"It was normal," he said with a shrug, "and it was awesome, knowing my dad was a superhero, kind of what some woman thinks of *me.*"

A gentle smile.

"But then he got hurt. Really hurt, and suddenly...it *wasn't* awesome."

That smile faded. "It was scary."

"Yeah."

Her hand smoothed over his chest.

"It rocked my world," he admitted. "I thought he was invincible, and when he almost died, it changed everything. He got better, of course"—since he was still around and healthy and whole—"but it was touch and go there for a while, and when he went back to working undercover, went back to being away, I worried myself sick, literally *sick*, every single time he was gone."

"Oh, honey," she whispered.

"My mom finally dragged me to a therapist to talk shit out, and it got better, but"—he brought her closer—"I would never leave someone, especially someone I care about, hanging like that." He brushed his lips across her forehead. "I honestly thought that we'd talked about it, otherwise I would have woken you up and—"

"It's okay," she murmured, stroking his jaw. "I get it now."

He studied her face, turned over her words in his mind, but he didn't detect anything in them aside from the truth, and considering he made a lot of his living from being able to discern fact from bullshit, that told him a lot.

"I'm sorry, baby," he said.

"It's okay." Her lips curved. "I'm sorry I threw yarn at you."

Chance ran his thumb along that curve. "I'm not. Now you've impressed me with your aim, so I have something else to admire about you." She giggled and he bent, snagged the basket she'd been holding when he'd walked into the shop. "So, are you going to tell me the truth or not?"

Her expression sobered. "About wh-what?" she stuttered.

He couldn't hold back his grin, even though he tried to by burying his face in her throat, flicking his tongue over the skin. "About your obsession with wicker?"

She was still.

So still for a heartbeat.

And then she swatted at his shoulder. "Just for that, I'm not going to give you any of the cupcakes I have to bake tonight."

His head straightened. "Cupcakes?"

"That's right," she said. "I have to make cupcakes for the bake sale at the elementary school tomorrow, chocolate fudge with chocolate buttercream frosting."

His stomach rumbled. "I'm an excellent taste tester."

"Uh-uh," she began saying, shaking her head. "Not going to change my mind. Me and my wicker obsession are going to go home alone, bake my cupcakes, and ignore the man who clearly doesn't understand the finer arts of woven materials."

He kissed her.

No holds barred. Lots of tongue and teeth and long enough for his lungs to start burning.

"I'll buy you dinner," he said when he managed to pull away. "You make the cupcakes. I eat one, just to make sure they're not poisoned."

Misty's eyes flew open.

Her lips parted.

Her head began to shake.

Then she busted out laughing.

It was the best thing he'd heard in two weeks.

11

DOUBLE FUDGE

Misty

HE SWIPED a finger in the bowl in front of her and gave her a smile that was so "aw shucks" that she didn't smack him with the whisk she was using to make the frosting.

"You better have washed your hands," she warned.

"I did."

He reached again, this time with another finger (as in one of the other nine fingers that hadn't been in his mouth).

But this time, she swatted him.

"No more," she ordered. "You'll ruin your dinner."

"I promise you, I won't," he said. "I could bathe in that frosting."

She put down her whisk and set up her piping bag in a glass (for easy filling). "Make yourself useful," she said, seeing him reach for the bowl again as if she couldn't see him, "and hold that bowl for me. If you keep your fingers out of it until I get the frosting in the bag, you can lick it."

"Really?"

A chuckle bubbled up in her throat. "Why do you sound like a ten-year-old little boy?"

"Because I feel like one?" he said. "My mom had six of us to take care of, and all of us had hollow legs, including Soph. She didn't have time to make anything from scratch, least of all cupcakes and frosting."

"Never?" Misty asked.

"You have five boys and one daughter, and you think you'd have time to be Betty Crocker?"

"I think I'd barely have time to sleep," she said, nodding at him to grip the bowl, one hand on the scraper the other on the opposite side of the plastic to get some purchase for scooping out the frosting. "Let alone have time to worry about making anything from scratch."

"Then you and my mom would be on the same page," he said.

Also, this just in, one bonus to him holding the bowl for her scraping was that he was close. Really close.

Close enough that she could smell him—all man and spice—feel the warmth from his body—and that was nice—and...well, just being close to him was really freaking great.

And yes, she knew that didn't go well with her rhyming theme.

But he was close.

She liked him close.

And she believed him when he said that he had meant to tell her that he'd be gone for a couple of weeks. Not just because of the fact that he was Soph's brother and wouldn't want to complicate things between their families, but because his words had been true, his expression pained when she'd told him he'd hurt her.

Maybe he was an Oscar-worthy actor.

But she didn't think he could fake something like that, didn't think he would have shared the story he had, if he wasn't telling the truth.

So, she was going to let it go.

Same as she had let the frosting stealing go.

Plus, he'd been genuinely surprised she was hurt when he'd come into the shop. She'd watched his smile melt away by her reaction—aka that of a pissed-off female—seen the confusion on his face. It was just that she'd been too furious to clearly track it before.

And the past couple of hours had been like their date.

Easy.

Perfect.

He'd helped her pick up the yarn she'd launched at him, righted the basket she'd dropped before loading it onto the proper shelf. Then they'd worked together to shelve the rest of her order—well, he'd taken care of that so she didn't have to get the step ladder from the back, and she'd put together the packets of materials she needed for the class she was teaching the following afternoon (an after-school session with some local Cub Scouts—yes, Cub Scouts, because their den leader was the shit and when one of the boys had expressed an interest in knitting, she hadn't made it a boy or girl thing—though there were boys *and* girls in the den Misty was teaching the next day—she'd just called Misty, set up a den meeting at the shop, and now the kids were going to learn something they might not have otherwise been exposed to).

After she locked up and closed out her cash drawer, putting the contents in the safe, he'd followed her back to her place then had pulled out his cell, and ordered up dinner. Also, side note, the man was a freaking master—he'd offered her three choices and let her pick, not leading with just, "What do you want to eat?" He'd given her concrete options that hadn't made her feel weird or bossy about making a selection.

Then he'd followed her orders in the kitchen.

Which were basically to stand there and look pretty.

Okay, they'd *been* "Stand there and look pretty."

So, he had—or at least, he had propped himself on the counter and watched her as she whipped up a double batch of her chocolate fudge cupcakes.

They were cooling on racks.

She had finished with the frosting.

They were waiting for their food to be delivered.

And not once had he seemed impatient, or like he wanted to be someplace else. Not once had he seemed anything other than interested in her. It was…addicting.

"Tell me about these cupcakes."

Brows drawing together, she glanced up at him. "What do you mean?"

"Why'd they ask you to make them?"

She smiled. "My friend Shannon substitute teaches at the elementary school on occasion. She used to teach third grade but only fills in if they're in a pinch now. Her daughter, however, is a full-time Dragon and is all in on the current fundraiser. They're raising money for a new playground. She likes my cupcakes." Misty buffed her knuckles on her collarbone over her shirt. "Just saying, *everyone* loves my cupcakes. So anyway, she asked. I like kids. I want them to have a new playground, so I'm making them."

"How much do they sell for?"

"Two bucks each."

His brows lifted. "That's gonna take a lot of cake."

More laughter in her throat, curving her lips as she guided him into putting the bowl down. He set it in the sink but didn't move away, leaning a hip against the counter next to her while scooping up more frosting on his finger and licking it up. She tore her eyes away—because seriously, that tongue was a glorious thing—and focused on what he said. "That is true. But really the bake sale on a whole is just an excuse to sugar up the kids, turn them loose with their friends, and then con the parents into B.S.ing, getting competitive, and spending money at the silent auction."

"So, cake, competition, and then more *cake*."

"Of the monetary variety?"

He winked. "Exactly."

Grinning, she lifted the now-filled piping bag out of the glass, twisting the end to seal it up, and headed to the racks of cupcakes. After checking to make sure they were cool, she started piping large swirls on top.

Chance fell quiet.

Or maybe she did, getting into the rhythm of icing the cupcakes.

Distantly, she heard the doorbell ring, heard Chance's soft, "I'll get it," before his footsteps drifted away. But she was firmly into her piping bag, getting those swirls perfect, putting the perfect pinch of sprinkles on top.

Then she was done.

Rolling her shoulders, she glanced around the kitchen and found it quiet and empty. The lights were on, but the counter Chance had been propping up was empty.

She figured he was still getting the food or setting it out—it didn't take *that* long to ice four dozen cupcakes. Though, she'd made five because she wasn't sure how many he would eat. After pulling out her cupcake carriers, she quickly loaded them up, stacking them safely in her fridge. They took up most of the open space, but that was okay. She hadn't had a chance to go to the grocery store, and with them ordering in food, it wasn't like she had to cook anything.

Wiping her hands on a towel, she wandered into the hallway.

The light was on in her living room, the TV buzzing quietly. A bag sat on her coffee table, its contents spread out on the surface, though the containers of their food still had the lids on, and Chance...

Chance was on her couch, socked feet propped on the table, and...he was asleep.

12

CLOUDLESS

Chance

HE WOKE up with an aching back and no idea where he was.

Sunlight was streaming in through the windows, his boots had been removed, and a blanket was tucked securely around him.

Blinking, he rubbed a hand over his jaw.

Misty's place.

Of course.

He'd been tired after the job, but that wasn't anything out of the ordinary. Two weeks in the shit meant that he'd need a couple of days to recuperate. Still, he hadn't been feeling that fatigued, or not enough to put off seeing Misty, nor did he remember it creeping in during their time together in the kitchen. He'd enjoyed watching her move around her space, talking to herself as she measured, answering his questions, asking him her own.

It had felt comfortable, an extension of that first night.

Of course, he'd wanted to steal that bowl of delicious icing and spend the night smearing it on and then licking it off her body.

But…the children.

The last thing he remembered was grabbing the food delivery, setting it up on the table, and then peeking back into the kitchen to see Misty almost done frosting.

He'd sat on the couch, turned on a hockey game, and had decided to give her a few minutes to finish up.

And now this.

He'd passed out on her.

Fuck.

Thrusting a hand through his hair, he sat up.

"Hey," came a soft voice.

He saw Misty standing in the kitchen, looking fucking adorable in a short pink robe, her hair in tangles, bringing a mug of coffee to her lips.

"Cloudless," he murmured, coming to his feet and crossing over to her. "I'm sorry."

She smiled. "It's—" Then that smile faded as he moved closer, snagging the mug from her hands, and plunking it on the counter. "Um—"

He kissed her.

Long and deep and slow, giving her the goodnight kiss he'd intended to leave her with as a good morning one instead.

Releasing her, cock throbbing, lungs sawing, he picked up her mug and handed it back to her.

He turned to the fridge, opened the door, and attempted to catalog the ingredients available for him to cook her breakfast around all the trays of cupcakes.

Fuck, he'd missed out on conning her out of one of those last night, too.

"Chance?"

"Hmm?" He opened a drawer, found a pound of bacon.

"Whatcha doing?"

"Making you breakfast," he said, grabbing a carton of eggs.

"Um."

"What?" he asked, turning to face her, setting both on the

counter and moving back toward her. She was flushed, that bottom lip swollen, tempting him into kissing her again.

"You're making me breakfast?" The question was utterly befuddled.

Was it because it was morning and she was always befuddled during this time of day? Or was it because he hadn't disappeared, was sticking around, and was cooking for her?

"Yes," he said, deciding that neither of the answers mattered.

He dropped a kiss to the tip of her nose, started rummaging in the drawers below the stove, unearthing a griddle and a frying pan for the eggs.

"Oh."

She blinked and the befuddlement was gone. "Do you want coffee?"

"Definitely."

Her lips curved and she moved to a cupboard, opening it. He got a glance at the shelves, saw they were absolutely crammed full of mismatched coffee mugs, watched as she selected one with apparent care.

"Cream and sugar?" she asked.

A shake of his head. "Just black."

Ducking, she sidled over to the coffee pot, filled his mug with the black brew, then set it near his elbow as he was cracking eggs.

"You're good at that."

He grinned, and since she was close, took the opportunity to kiss her nose again. "Had to get good at a lot of things when I lived on my own."

"So cooking was one?"

A nod. "Cooking was one."

"What else was one?"

"Laundry. Cleaning. Making my own doctor's appointments."

"Who decided you needed to get good at it?"

His brows drew together. "Me."

"I don't believe it."

His gaze shot to hers, brows lifting now, but she stared back at him with suspicion written into the lines of her face...until her lips began tilting up at the corners. "What?" he asked.

Those lips curved fully; laughter tinkled through the room. Sunshine and a bright, clear sky.

"What is it, Cloudless?" he asked, wiping his hands on a towel before he dropped them to her waist, scooped her up and plunked her on the counter, stepping between her legs.

"It's just that I'm such a dork." She shrugged, shook her head. "I was trying to tease you and it's not really funny, and I'm—" Now she groaned. "I'm just *such* a dork, laughing at my own jokes and—" She glanced up at his face. "Now I'm not making any sense, I know."

"What was funny?" A beat. "To you."

Misty winced. "A man making his own doctor's appointments...of his own volition."

Chance went still, then started busting up, dropping his head to her shoulder as his laughter filled the space between them.

"What?" she asked when he caught his breath.

He lifted his head. "Ask me how many times in his life my dad has made his own doctor's appointments."

"Um..." Her mouth was parted, tempting him again. Her cheeks flushed.

"Zero," he murmured, dropping his head, darting his tongue over her bottom lip.

It took a second for his reply to penetrate, but then she started smiling again.

"Cloudless," he whispered.

Her breath slid out of her. "Why do you keep calling me that?"

Because she was the cloudless sky after an eternity of being shrouded by shadows, the clearing horizon after a storm. She was sweet and bright and for the first time in his life, he wanted to keep a woman, even if that might mean facing some of those fears from his childhood. Namely, that he never wanted to create a family that might be left behind, left worrying at home, left alone if something happened to him.

He'd been careful of distance, careful to keep things casual and light, so fucking cognizant of the risk of tying someone to him when he did the job he did.

But that one date with Misty had him thinking that having someone waiting at home might be all the more motivation to return safely, to get the job done quickly and smartly and then get back to the bright, cloudless skies his woman gave him.

Chance kissed her nose again, chewing on that thought, knowing it was true, and went back to cracking eggs.

"You're not going to tell me?"

"Nope." He found a fork, ignoring the noise of protest she made, and got scrambling. Once they were good, he returned to the fridge for some milk and cheese, both of which he added to the bowl. Bacon on the griddle, eggs whisked and ready. "What do you have on the agenda today?"

Her nostrils flared when she inhaled, her narrow eyes fixed on him.

Then she seemed to realize he wasn't going to budge, even with the adorable glare she was tossing his way, because she sighed and said, "I need to drop the cupcakes at school then go open the shop. I've got a class in the afternoon with a bunch of nine-year-old boys and girls, then two more—a beginner and an advanced course. Then I need to make an appearance at the bake sale, do the requisite schmoozing, and pick up my cupcake holders. *Then* I need to go back to the shop and prep for my classes tomorrow. Whew," she added, smiling up at him. "And now I'm tired even though the day has hardly begun."

"What can I do to help you?"

She froze.

"Are you going to ask *what* again?" He tugged a lock of her hair before turning the bacon on the griddle. "Because I think it's cute, but I also think it's obvious, honey. I've got a couple of days off. I came back to Stoneybrook to spend them with you. So, I'm selfish. I want to take advantage of our time together."

"Wouldn't it be better if you spent your vacation at home?"

"In Atlanta?"

She nodded.

"No."

"Um..."

"I've already decided I'm moving up to Stoneybrook, Cloudless. Decided it a while ago. Mom and Dad are close, and Soph is here. My brothers aren't far away either, and certainly a fuck-ton closer than me living several states away."

"But your work."

"Told you, I'd already planned to move into the area, as my work takes me up this way far more often than not. Which I've made certain of since I've been planning on moving to Stoney-brook for a while, and aside from a few cases that I'll need to travel back and forth for, most of my work and connections are in this area." He turned back to the bacon, saw it was nearly done, and dumped the eggs in the pan. "I'll always have an odd case or two on the burner that will require me to travel, but while I love my work, I also like being nearby and connected to the people I care about."

She was quiet, and when he slanted a look in her direction, he saw her shoulders rise and fall on a breath.

But when it became apparent that she wasn't going to talk, he focused on the eggs and said, "Just in case you were uncertain after things went down two weeks ago, I put you in the category of people I care about."

Another breath.

Another rise and fall of her shoulders.

"Um..."

Fuck, now she was being cute again, and now he had to kiss her again, and that meant risking the bacon and eggs, and for all his talk of being a functioning adult—including his ability to cook for himself—eggs and bacon was pretty much the only thing he could make for breakfast, aside from toast, cereal, and oatmeal, and he didn't think those were quite "cooking."

"Cloudless," he warned.

She blinked up at him.

Fuck it.

He'd risk the bacon and eggs.

He bent and kissed her.

And no surprise, forgot about the food, forgot about trying to keep his "cooking" skills under wraps. He got lost in the cute and soft and sweet, then got lost in the way she leaned against him, her breasts against his chest, her thighs around his hips, her tongue meeting his.

She moaned, and he lost it, sweeping her up into his arms and dropping her onto the kitchen island. He yanked at the tie on her robe, tugging the pink fabric off her shoulders and exposing the thin tank top and panties she wore beneath.

Hard nipples, pressing against the white fabric, breasts pillowing over the low neckline.

Soaked underwear, so fucking wet that the fabric was nearly see-through, or at least giving him a glimpse of pink folds beneath.

His mouth watered, and for a moment he couldn't decide if wanted it on her breasts or her pussy.

Then she released a shuddering breath, jiggling those tits, and he moved. Nudging the pencil-thin straps down her arms, he yanked the stretchy material. It resisted for a moment, then her breasts popped free.

He bent and sucked a nipple deep. Her fingers came to his head, wove into his hair, gripping him tightly and holding him against her as he used teeth and tongue and suction to drive her wild. Hips bucking against him, hands clenched in his hair, nipple so freaking hard. His name tumbled off her lips as he released her, as he kissed his way to her other breast and suckled. At the same time, he snaked a hand down beneath the waistband of her underwear, spearing it through her folds and slipping two fingers inside her, using his palm against her clit just the way he'd discovered she liked.

"*Oh,*" she moaned, gripping tight at his hair, lifting him from her breast. "Inside," she begged. "Inside me."

Yes.

Yes.

He wanted that.

Reaching down, he unbuttoned his jeans, yanked down the zipper, and pulled out his cock. An arm around her waist, hefting her up enough to tug off her panties. He stepped between her thighs, started to press home into all that hot, wet tightness.

Wet.

Wet.

"Fuck," he growled, trying to go slow, even though that was fucking torture.

"No," Misty groaned, gripped his ass, trying to press him deeper.

"Trying not to come, baby." He fumbled for his control. "Trying not to fuck you too hard."

She pulled him in again. "I like hard."

"You deserve sweet," he said.

Her tits were bouncing in time to her rapid breathing. "Yes." Each word was punctuated by a breath. "But I want you to fuck me hard."

And that was when he stopped fumbling for control.

He lost it altogether, yanking her toward him as she ordered, "Now."

That he could do.

He pressed home, the wet, tight heat of her surrounding his cock, sucking him in, pulsing around her. So fucking hard. He didn't think he'd ever been this turned on, this close to exploding with one fucking stroke under his belt.

The only consolation was that Mist was right there with him, her hips jerking up toward his, her hands pulling him in. "More. Harder," she chanted, over and over again.

He moved faster, harder, pounding into her, knowing he wasn't going to last long.

His fingers went to her clit, pressing hard as he thrusted deep, not showing her any mercy when she moaned and jerked. This wasn't a gentle ascent. He was about to tumble over the edge and so he was yanking her up alongside him, not letting her slow, not going easy and gentle.

Her body went stiff. "*Chance.*"

The fracture was in her voice, in his name.

She was close, thank fucking God.

He pounded into her, harder and faster, feeling his own orgasm singeing its way up his spine.

"*Chance,*" she moaned again.

And he felt her start to convulse around him, her pussy clenching him tight, and now she was yanking him up, thrusting them both over the cliff into oblivion.

She exploded.

He was right there with her.

Pleasure spiraling out through his body, making his legs wobble and shake, forcing himself to brace against the island, or else take them both to the tile floor.

"Holy hell," she breathed.

"I second that," he murmured, kissing her bare shoulder.

They stood there for a minute, his cock still hard and buried deep, their breathing slowly evening out.

Then she sniffed.

Then *he* sniffed.

His gaze darted to the stove, toward the black smoke rising off the griddle, the frying pan, filling the kitchen with it.

"Fuck," he hissed.

The smoke detectors went off, blaring through the house.

What a goddamned clusterfuck.

But then Misty grinned, her mouth coming up to find his. "I've got another pound of bacon in the freezer."

Okay, he could revise his previous thought.

Not a clusterfuck.

Not even remotely close.

Not when he had this woman in his arms, in his life.

"Bacon," he said, slipping out and helping her down.

She was still smiling when she said, "Freezer."

"Smartass." A kiss to her nose.

"*Hungry* smartass."

He smacked that ass, smart or not, moved to the stove and turned it off, yanked the pans off the heat. "Go clean up. I'll take care of breakfast."

Her grin turned into a smirk, but she simply righted her tank, picked up her panties and robe, and turned for the bedroom.

Chance snagged her arm, tugged her back to him.

He'd take care of breakfast.

He just needed to taste that smirk first.

So, he did.

13

SCHOOL TONGUE

Misty

"Going to tell me what's going on with *that?*" her friend Shan asked, nudging Misty with her shoulder and nodding to their right.

Well, Misty's right.

Shan's left.

Because her friend had cornered her the moment Chance had gotten drawn into conversation with Shan's significant other, Finn (only one of the biggest movie stars in the world, no big deal), and their daughter (Shan's biological, Finn's adopted since Shan's ex was the biggest tool bag on the planet, and Finn had never seen Rylie as anything but his).

To her credit, Misty didn't pretend to not know who Shan was talking about.

For one, Shan wouldn't let her get away with pretending, and that would only draw out the interrogation.

For another, Misty wanted to share.

Needed to get it off her chest.

"*That's* Chance."

"Yes," Shan said, waving her hand through the air. "I know

all about Soph's brother *and* your date, which was supposedly fabulous, according to Soph, but what your sister-in-law *didn't* see these last two weeks, since she's on a freaking private island, is that you've been moping around like someone set your yarn collection on fire."

Misty shuddered, that thought too horrible to bear. "Not funny," she said. "And also, you've spent plenty of time on private islands yourself."

Shan grinned, something that had been absent on her friend's gorgeous face far too often before she met Finn. "That's true. Also, nice try at distraction."

She wasn't really going for distraction, though she couldn't deny that her half of the conversation up to that point had brought it. "I like him, Shan. A lot. Too much, considering we've had one and a half dates and I spent our reunion yesterday pelting him with skeins of yarn and yelling at him in equal measures."

"One and a *half?*"

"Yup." She was considering last night only half a date, considering only *half* of them were awake.

Shan's brows lifted. "Explain."

So, she did.

About the date—the escape room through to dinner, including the fabulous sex, the way she'd felt complete in a way she had never expected, especially after one evening together. Then she told Shan about the morning after and her being so damned hurt about him not sticking around, how he'd been gone for two weeks on the job, him showing up at the shop, his shock and then his explanation and apology. Finally, she told her friend about him hanging out with her while she'd baked cupcakes, how he'd licked the bowl and ordered dinner and then had fallen asleep on the couch, not wanting to disturb her. She dished about that morning, the way it was so easy for her to talk to him, the burned breakfast, and the kitchen island sex.

"Wow," Shan murmured. "Make sure you disinfect that before you have me over for dinner next time."

Misty swatted her friend. "Asshole."

Shan grinned. "I need kitchen island sex."

"Isn't countertop sex what got you pregnant the second time?"

That grin didn't fade. "Yes. Or at least I think so. But no reason it can't do the job again."

Misty's heart leaped. "You're thinking of trying again?"

Shan bit her lip, nodded. "We're past the thinking stage."

Misty squealed. "Seriously?"

Shan nodded again. "We've lost it, haven't we?"

"In the best freaking way possible," Misty assured her. "You and Finn are fabulous parents." She did some shoulder nudging of her own. "And I imagine that trying is half the fun."

That got Shannon grinning. "Damn right it is."

"Especially when you're married to a big ol' movie star."

"That too." Shan sobered. "You good though, honey? That was a shitty thing for him to have done, leaving without a word. You believe him when he said that he truly thought he told you?"

Misty paused to consider that even though her ready answer had her wanting to immediately say, "Yes, of course, I believe him." But she owed it to herself—and Chance—to truly consider that. Because if some part of her had been swept up in him the day before, in the attraction, the power of his charm, and if that part of her didn't truly believe his explanation, then what they were building might be destined for failure.

So, she took the time.

She thought and pondered and thought again.

And then she met her friend's stare, knowing that the words she was speaking came from her heart. "I saw his face. I saw how distraught he was when he realized I'd been hurt," she said. "And I know how he treated me on our date, last night, and this morning. I know him being Soph's brother and me being Rob's sister complicates things. He loves his family, loves his sister. He wouldn't want to hurt me, just for that alone. And," she whispered, blinking when Shan grabbed her hand and squeezed, oddly touched and near tears, "he wouldn't want to hurt me. Because he cares about me. *Me.*"

The last was said with some wonder.

Not that Misty thought she was unworthy of that.

But because she felt the same about him.

She *cared.*

"Well," Shan said, blinking and looking near tears herself. "I like the way he looks at you."

Misty smiled. "There's that."

Shan leaned in. "And I like the way he noticed that you're about to burst into tears, even though he was deep in conversation with my very sexy husband, and he's already heading this way."

"What—?" Misty started to turn to look for him, but then a pair of arms were around her, lips were pressed to her jaw.

"You okay?" was the soft question in her ear.

Shan smirked. "I'll go grab your cupcake holders."

A shiver slid through her, Chance's warm chest pressed to her back, as though he thought she was cold and needed his warmth, rather than his words in her ear, that small touch of his mouth had her shuddering, her pussy throbbing. She tried not to melt into him. Tried and failed, that was. Because he was there and his strong body was big and surrounding hers, and… it was wonderful. Clearing her throat, she shook herself out of her fog and caught Shan's arm. "But the cake auction hasn't started yet."

Shan pecked her on the cheek. "And you're not going to be here for it."

Chance chuckled.

Her friend's gaze drifted over Misty's shoulder, and narrowed, presumably on Chance's. "You hurt her again, you answer to me."

Mist felt Chance nod.

Shan repeated the gesture then turned away again. "Going to get those holders," she said.

They were quiet as Shan moved away, Rylie skipping over to take her mom's hand, Finn and baby trailing behind. Misty spun in Chance's arms. "You got the patented Teacher Look from Shan."

His mouth hitched up. "That I did."

She winced. "Sorry about that. Shan is a good friend and—"

He bent, pressed his smiling lips to hers for a kiss that wasn't full of tongue and heat, but one that was long and intense enough that she knew—based on their location (the school auditorium) and based on the percentage of the population of Stoneybrook currently in said auditorium (a solid seventy-five percent)—everyone would be talking about her and Chance and The Kiss.

But The Kiss was so good that Misty found she didn't care.

At least until a growl sounded behind them and she all but jumped out of her skin. Chance just swept his thumb over her bottom lip, barely flinching when Finn—the source of the growl; apparently he was feeling protective—jabbed Chance in the side with the stack of cupcake holders. Shan was behind him, arms wrapped around their littlest munchkin, Rylie having run off somewhere.

Chance released her, took the cupcake holders, somehow managing to tuck them under one arm while threading the fingers of his free hand through hers (something that would also get the gossips talking).

Her friend's expression was smug, and she waved her fingers in goodbye as she tugged a narrow-eyed Finn away.

"Let's get you back to your shop," Chance murmured, "get your shit done so I can have you to myself."

"My stuff isn't shit."

He froze, mouth tipping up at the corners as she glared at him. His fingers squeezed hers. "Let's get your *stuff* done."

Now it was her turn to smile.

To squeeze his fingers.

To rise on tiptoe and slant her mouth across his.

And for the record, *her* kiss had tongue. A school-appropriate amount of tongue.

But still tongue, and enough of it that when she rocked back onto her heels, saw that Chance looked slightly dazed, she knew *her* expression was smug. Especially when she said, "Let's get my shit done and go home."

Silence.

One beat of long, taut silence.

And then Chance started laughing.

Best sound *ever*.

———

"LIKE THIS?" Chance asked, just over an hour later.

She grinned. "Is it killing you to be wrapped in pink yarn?"

He shot her a look, repeated, "Like this?"

It was killing him. Maybe not as much as the purple laced with slender threads of gold had, when she'd had him be her measuring tool. But it was torturing him in a way that promised he'd get retribution later.

And she had a feeling that she'd like his retribution, given the heat in his green eyes.

She spread his hands a little farther apart then started wrapping the yarn around it. "I used to do this for my mom."

Those green eyes hit hers. "Yeah?"

"Yeah," she whispered.

"It must have been hard to lose them both."

"I miss them a lot," she said by way of agreement, "but I had Rob and Carmella"—Rob's former wife, who'd passed just over three years before—"and Carmella's family is great. They looked out for me and Rob. After she died, they took it hard.

Obviously," she added, because who wouldn't take the death of their daughter hard?

"A lot of loss in a short amount of time."

"Yeah," she whispered again.

"Strong even in the face of a storm," he murmured, his voice a soft rasp in the quiet of the shop. "That storm blew through, and you still found a way to be happy and successful."

She blinked. "Chance."

"Cloudless," he murmured.

She blinked again, realized he was giving her the explanation he hadn't before. "*Chance.*"

"Won't ever forgive myself for hurting you," he said softly, his long, tan fingers wrapped in pink yarn.

Another blink.

And then she lost it.

Tears slipping out of the corners of her eyes, a sob hitching her breathing.

He lost the yarn, tugged her into his arms, pressing her against all those strong lines of his chest, his warm body surrounding her as tears cascaded down her face. "I'm sorry, sweetheart." His voice was gravel. His hold tight. "I'm so sorry—"

She finally got herself together enough to suck in a breath. "Stop," she whispered. "*Stop,*" she said a little more clearly. "I'm not upset about that." Another inhale to get her breathing under control. "I'm *not,*" she repeated when his face remained grave. "I'm not upset *at all.*"

His brow lifted.

She had the insane urge to laugh.

So, she did.

And then she shook her head, got herself together, and stopped the tears, the laughter. She cupped Chance's face in her palms. "I'm not upset," she said. "I'm a crier, which I'm guessing you get by now, but by being a crier, I mean I'm a crier under any circumstance, but most especially when a man I really like gives me sweet words without reservation, and calls me Cloudless, and says I'm strong. Which I get"—she pushed some of her hair out of her face—"is sort of eliminated by the fact that I started crying because of it. But"—a shrug—"I'm a crier. I cry when I'm happy and sad and in between. I cry at Shark Week shows and SPCA commercials. I cried when Soph brought me some yarn back from Turkey when she was filming that movie. And I'll *definitely* cry when a sweet man tells me something wonderful."

"Mist," he rasped.

She sniffed. "Fair warning, I'll probably also cry when you say my name like that."

He nudged her palms off his face, cupped her jaw in turn, thumb sweeping up to wipe her tears away, and then he stared at her for so long, his eyes fathomless and completely unreadable, his expression almost hard, that a pit began opening in her stomach.

Then everything went soft.

Emerald went molten.

His mouth curved.

And he said, "I guess I'm going to have to buy stock in Kleenex because I'm not done telling you all the wonderful things you are."

Misty froze.

His words hit.

And she started crying again.

Chance tugged her close for the second time in as many minutes, muttered, "Definitely investing in Kleenex."

Laughter blended with tears.

But Chance's arms never loosened.

14

DIAMONDS

Chance

"I'LL SEE YOU SOON," he murmured, sitting on the edge of Misty's bed three days later.

He'd intended to stay in Stoneybrook for a bit longer, wanting to find an apartment or house to rent, plus a space for his office, but he'd ended up spending every minute with Misty. And then every night—after that first one where he'd passed out on the couch—in her bed.

It had been awesome.

He hadn't wanted to be away from her, so he'd spent his time helping out in her shop. Well, not really helping too much, if he was honest. Yarn, as it turned out, wasn't exactly his thing.

But he'd offered his hands for her to wrap the balls when needed (though it turned out she actually had a tool for that, so it hadn't been too often, just at the end of the day, when it was just the two of them and they were talking about everything and nothing).

He'd learned how to run the register and sign people up for classes.

He'd hauled boxes around her storeroom.

But mostly, he'd pretended to work on his computer while sitting on a stool at her counter and spending the majority of his time watching her.

Committing her to memory.

The way her blond hair shone in the sunlight pouring through the windows in the morning. The freckles on her nose. How her eyes changed color depending on what she wore and what time of day it was.

Learning the small things.

Like how she had different smiles—one for customers, one for friends, one for customers who were friends, and one for…him.

Bar none, his was the best.

Probably because she'd been giving it to him a lot lately. Probably because she was giving it to him right then.

Because he'd learned.

He'd kept them up late the night before, worn her straight out. Her fault, since she'd disappeared into her closet after dinner and emerged wearing some sexy as shit contraption that was black and lace and revealed more than it hid—and that was about as much as he'd taken in before he'd pounced on her.

She'd been limp and flushed, her eyes barely open, mouth swollen, limbs sprawled on the mattress, and more asleep than awake by the time he finished with her.

So, it went without saying that he'd woken up before her.

Despite being pretty damned tired himself.

He'd slipped out of bed, left a note on the pillow next to hers, and had returned with coffee and cinnamon rolls.

The scent of the former roused her.

The latter had gotten him his smile.

She was easy to please, and fuck, was he looking forward to continuing to do it, and if things kept flowing the way they had between them, then he was looking forward to doing it for the rest of his life.

Now, she was still sleepy.

But she was full of coffee and cinnamon roll and didn't have to hit her granola bar basket.

Though, he couldn't lie. The granola bars in that wicker container were delicious, made in town by one of her friends, Frankie, who apparently owned a health food shop on Stoneybrook's main street, just two blocks from Tangled.

Still, the cinnamon rolls—decidedly *not* healthy—had the bars beat.

"Thanks for breakfast," she murmured, arching her back and stretching her arms over her head in a way that wasn't intentionally sexy, but sure as shit was anyway. Especially when she was naked beneath that sheet and her breasts were only inches from exposure.

And if he caught a glimpse of them...

Well, he would be late getting on the road and investigating the lead that had come up for a case he was working—an oxycontin ring a small PD had contracted with him to investigate. He'd worked with the DEA and FBI on closing such rings, and now his specialty had become aiding small-town police departments or sheriff's offices to get a handle on distribution. Heroin and fentanyl and oxy were fucking with communities, especially those without the resources that bigger cities had.

He went under. He gathered information and evidence. He turned that over to the detectives.

They closed the case.

Often to fanfare that left his involvement out.

Which suited him fine.

He did what he did because he was good at it, because it was important, because it helped people. Cruising under the media's radar was just an added bonus.

"You're welcome," he said, tearing his gaze away from her tempting body, the nipples just barely contained beneath the sheet. "Hope you really do love those cinnamon rolls, because they may have been the best thing I've ever eaten, so we'll be getting them often."

Her expression went mischievous. "You like them even more than the pulled pork sandwiches I made you last night?" she asked archly.

Those pulled pork sandwiches with homemade coleslaw had him contemplating diamond rings, they were so good.

"No fucking way."

She grinned. "Smart answer."

"I *can* be smart occasionally."

Her face softened then went contrite. "I think a lot more than occasionally. I'm sorry I said you were stupid the other day. I—"

"I know, Cloudless. Don't think of it for another second, okay?"

She nibbled on her bottom lip. Then nodded. "Okay, baby." Holding the sheet to her chest, she sat up and cuddled close to his side, changing the subject, "Will you be able to talk this time?" Misty asked. "Or should I just plan to see you when you get back?"

God, she was sweet.

He smoothed back her sleep-mussed hair. "I should be able to talk. You call or text when you have time"—he'd given her his number the moment things were settled between them—"and if I don't pick up, I'll call or text back as soon as I can." He gently loosened a tangle in her hair. "Plus, this isn't undercover. I'll be in a hotel at night and should have plenty of time to talk then, if you want to hear from me."

Tiger's eyes on his. "I want to hear from you."

No games. No prevaricating. Just putting it out there.

Fuck, he wanted to kiss her.

He wanted to strip that sheet away.

But...work. Get the job done, chase down the lead, come back to Misty, and spend many hours in bed giving her orgasms. Mentally, he nodded to himself.

Good plan.

He pressed a kiss to her forehead, started to stand. "I'll be in contact as much as I can."

"Okay."

Feet turning toward the door, he forced himself to keep moving.

Ten feet. Five. Two. On the threshold.

"Chance?"

He didn't turn from the door. "Yeah?"

"Kiss me one more time before you go?"

He could do that.

Spinning, preparing himself for a chaste press of her lips to his, he froze when she tossed the sheet to the side, exposing that naked body he was addicted to. His cock twitched. His hands clenched into fists.

And then he was moving.

Back to the bed.

Scooping her up into his arms.

Slanting his mouth over hers. Not chastely.

Rolling to his back so all her glorious curves were pressed to his.

She didn't hesitate, just met him kiss for kiss, and when they needed air, he broke away from her mouth and focused his attention on her breasts. They were hanging in his face, so freaking close to his lips, his teeth, his tongue, so how could he not?

Her moans might be his favorite sound in the world.

"Chance," she breathed, her fingers digging into his hair when he suckled her deeply, her hips bucking against him.

Okay, maybe her moans were second to the sound of his name on her lips.

She released him when he switched breasts, reaching between them to undo the button of his jeans, yank down the zipper. He lifted his hips enough so that she could push them down, still sucking on her nipple, caressing her other breast.

Her wet pussy brushed his cock.

Once. Twice.

He released her breast, snagged her hips, and coaxed her down.

"You told me you like to be on top—" He groaned when all that tight, wet heat surrounded him.

"I told you," she panted, slowly grinding down on him, "that it's easier for me to—*ah*—" She bottomed out. "It's easier for me to *come* on top," she finished, her eyes sliding closed. "That's it. That's—" She broke off again, hips jerking as she started moving, a groan tumbling off her tongue.

"Then make it easy, Cloudless."

Her eyes met his.

She smiled.

Then she took herself into oblivion.

And he was happy to just cruise over after her.

15

BASEBALL BATS

Misty

"You're amazing!" Soph said as they sat on hers and Rob's back deck.

They'd just spent two weeks on the beach, and yet Soph had spent the better part of their dinner staring out at the waves.

Her sister-in-law loved the ocean.

And Misty couldn't blame her. It was gorgeous, especially the soft sand and gentle waves that were party to Stoneybrook's stretch of ocean.

"You like it?" she asked.

Soph held up the blanket Misty hadn't been able to stop herself from knitting—a pretty purple ombre that matched a sweater her brother had conned Misty out of coughing up (even though she'd been planning on keeping it for herself). The sweater looked a million times better on Soph than it would have on Misty, and truthfully, Soph loved it more than Misty ever could.

Namely because Misty's closet was plumb full of sweaters, and she didn't appreciate her work as much as Soph did.

Case in point, Soph was wearing it that evening.

So, Mist got an up close and personal view of how good of a job she did matching the ombre.

Spoiler alert: she did an *excellent* job.

"I love it!" Soph said, setting the blanket on the table and sweeping Misty up into a hug. "Thank you so much."

This was why she loved Soph for Rob.

Why she loved Soph, straight up.

She was a Hollywood actor, one of the most well-known A-listers in the world. And she was genuinely excited about a blanket. Misty knew she made good blankets. They were well-crafted with quality materials—like everything in her shop—but Soph could probably get a twenty-four-carat gold blanket for free (though that would be both heavy and not very cuddly). Hell, if such a blanket existed, some well-meaning product manager had probably already sent one to Soph's agent.

Yet despite all that—the free stuff, the movie sets, the over-the-top fans, and paparazzi—Soph was normal.

"This is the first baby gift we've gotten," she squealed in Misty's ear. "Oh my God. Why does it feel so real now?" Her eyes were wide when she dropped her arms and stepped back. "Holy fuck. I'm going to be a mom." She turned to Rob. "We're going to be parents. *How* are we going to be parents? I don't know anything about being a mom. What if I fuck up?" She grabbed the blanket, held it to her chest like it was her pacifier. And maybe, in a way, it was. "Oh shit. We're going to fuck up. *I'm* going to fuck up."

Rob wrapped Soph in his arms, tucked her face into his chest, his head dropping, lips to her ears, murmuring something Misty couldn't hear.

Not that she was going to put herself in a position to eavesdrop.

Instead, she quietly gathered the glasses and plates from dinner, brought them into the kitchen, and washed up. Then she slipped out the front door and got into her car.

It had been four days since Chance had gone on his job, and

they'd talked every night, texted throughout the days. Apparently, the lead had been fruitful, so he'd stayed longer than planned before handing off the case to the detectives he'd worked with, giving his statement.

Thus, she hadn't heard from him for most of that day.

He was supposed to text her when he was heading back to Stoneybrook, though.

But he hadn't done that yet and considering he was about six hours away, she wasn't sure if she'd see him that evening.

Pouty lip time.

Sighing, she carefully—carefully!—backed out of the driveway, but instead of driving home and sitting on her couch missing Chance, she decided to stop by Tangled. She needed to place a large order the following day, which meant she had to do her favorite thing...not.

Inventory.

Sigh.

But she might as well get started on it. Better to distract herself with the mundane rather than pouting at home because she wanted Chance to be there.

Plus, she had a new audiobook she'd happily dive into for a couple of hours.

So, she parked in front of the shop—not bothering to worry about leaving the spots open for her customers like she normally did by parking in the alley out back. Downtown Stoneybrook was quiet at this late hour—late being almost nine o'clock—and the streets had rolled up nearly an hour before.

Especially on her side of downtown.

The restaurants—a couple of which even stayed open until nearly ten (gasp!)—were on the opposite end of Main Street. Tangled closed most nights at six, sometimes seven if she had a class, and her end of downtown was retail, most of which closed at five. Not to mention, the space next door had been empty for quite a while.

All that to say, it wasn't exactly hopping when she got out of her car.

She dug into her purse for her keys then tugged them out, unlocking the door to the shop and pushing inside before closing it and flicking the dead bolt behind her. Leaving the lights off, for fear of drawing attention (or Mrs. Hutchinson happening to drive by and seeing her inside), Mist moved into the back room, snagged her clipboard from the hook on the wall, and started going through her stores.

First the yarn, noting which of her most popular blends she was low on, which she was out of altogether (only one variety, since she tended to be an over-orderer, but she'd had a new client come in and clear her out on a gorgeous periwinkle merino blend to crochet a blanket for her grandmother). The yarn was always the most fun—she loved feeling it, stroking it, working with it—but the rest of the items (needles, hooks, baskets—and Chance would probably find that hilarious, considering what he thought of her basket obsession—patterns, scissors, and more) were also fun to order.

She liked to stock the basics, but it also fed her soul to order colorful, pretty items that she knew her customers would love as much as she did.

Case in point, a bedazzled crochet hook—size seven—and a bright purple knitting basket with hedgehogs on it.

One, sparkles.

Two, hedgehogs. Was there a cuter animal on the planet?

Convince her otherwise.

Ha.

Maybe a baby platypus or a pangolin.

But they didn't have pangolin-printed knitting baskets. Or at least, she hadn't come across one yet. Though, she did make a mental note to keep an eye out for one. A knitter never knew when she might need a pangolin-printed knitting basket. It was as simple as that.

Giggling to herself, she made a couple of notes on her clip-board and hung it up.

She was just pulling out her phone to turn off the audiobook blaring through her earbuds when she heard it.

Crash.

One loud enough that she heard it through the rumbling male voice playing on her earbuds. Frowning, she hit pause and the audiobook stopped.

Then she heard crunching.

Crunching?

What the hell?

She poked her head out the doorway and had to immediately stifle a gasp. There was someone in her shop, and the front door had been shattered.

It was safety glass.

It wasn't supposed to shatter like that.

But it had.

And she saw the reason why.

Fuck. She didn't dare say the word aloud, not when she saw the tall figure moving toward the register, a baseball held in his hand. The shadows were thick, and she was cursing herself for not having turned the lights on, risk of Mrs. Hutchinson or not.

She'd take the surly old bat over a baseball *bat* any day of the week.

The figure—she made a guess by the shape of the body—appeared male, though she couldn't see his face, and she supposed he could be a slender, tall female. But there was some-thing about the way he moved that screamed *man.*

Then he made it to the register, trying to force open the drawer and growling in a voice that was *definitely* male, and her suspicions were reinforced.

A man. Probably almost six feet. Slender though. She'd guess he was only twenty or thirty pounds heavier than her—so putting him at one-seventy or one-eighty. Enough weight on her that even her Wii Fit Kickboxing classes probably wouldn't do much to protect herself.

And protect?

Fuck, she had her phone in her hand.

Why wasn't she calling 9-1-1?

The door to the storeroom didn't have a lock, and if she wanted to get out the back door, she'd have to risk moving through the store and by that man with the scary bat.

A bat he now put to use wailing on the register, still trying to get the drawer open.

The cash was all locked in the safe.

He wouldn't get anything, not that him stealing petty cash was the top of her priorities. Namely, priority one was staying safe and alive and away from that baseball bat.

So, taking advantage of the noise he was making—and she was cringing at the sound of more shattering—this time of her glass cabinet where the register sat, and the register itself—she carefully shut the door, shoving a chair under the handle, and then shifting some of the heavier boxes next to it. She did this as she dialed the number for emergency services, holding the phone to her ear and whispering who she was and what was happening.

Hopefully, Stoneybrook being so boring would mean the response time was rapid.

Was instant.

Then the storefront went quiet, and she froze, setting down another box she'd been trying to use as a barricade as quietly as possible.

She flicked off the light, hoping the man on the other side wouldn't notice the sliver of light disappearing from beneath the door, and darted behind a stack of boxes, trying to cram herself into the shadows behind the old table she had stored there and the extra supplies.

"...Misty?" came the voice in her ear. "You there?"

"Yes," she breathed. "I can't talk."

Because she heard it then.

Footsteps.

Coming her way.

"He's coming," she whispered.

"Police on their way, Misty," the dispatcher said. "Stay calm."

The doorknob rattled.

"He's trying to get into the room where I'm at."

"Can you get out?"

A sob hitched in her throat, and she swallowed it down, unwilling to let the sound give her away. "No, I can't."

"Stay hidden, Misty. The police are on their way."

The knob stopped rattling and turned. The door started to push open, only to get stuck on the chair.

Please. Please, God, let it stop him.

Quiet.

It went quiet again.

She released a breath. "I think—"

The door exploded inward, the chair toppling backward, the boxes scattering. The noise made her jump, a scream lodging in her throat. Then she didn't have time to do anything.

The lights flicked on, blinding her for a moment.

And then the man was in front of her, bat raised.

Bat…descending.

She ducked, tried to dodge.

But she was too slow.

The world went fuzzy, and she fell to the floor.

16

MAIN STREET

Chance

HE'D FORGOTTEN to text Misty.

He'd gotten his shit done, hit the road, and then had immediately spent the better part of the drive on the phone, dealing with details for his last two remaining cases in Atlanta.

One, not drug-related but a favor to an old high school friend whose ex-husband was trying to fuck her over on child support payments. He'd gotten the break he needed the night before, his searches turning up plenty of money for those payments to be made, and he had to break the news, email her the information, and then arrange for her to meet the courier he'd set up so she could also bring paper copies of what he'd unearthed to her attorney.

Two, drug-related but also a favor. This one for a former client whose son was in a bad way, and she wanted to know if he was using.

He was.

Which meant that Chance had to break that news and try to do it gently.

But there wasn't an easy way to tell a woman who'd been a single mom to three kids, who'd gotten fucked over by her ex-husband, who'd struggled and fought her way to a good life, that her son was an addict and things with him weren't looking good.

That call had taken a while.

And after he'd let her cry it out, did his best to comfort her, even though it was fucking difficult to comfort someone over the phone, he'd driven in silence for a bit.

Then he'd turned on the radio, lost himself in some music.

Then he'd remembered he was supposed to text Misty.

By then he'd been forty-five minutes from Stoneybrook and figured he'd surprise her by showing up at her house, and if she wasn't back from Rob and Soph's house—where he knew they'd been having dinner together, something that would also be a perk of moving to town, actually getting to see his sister on the regular (and getting to be an awesome uncle to his soon-to-be niece or nephew)—he'd go to Soph's place and play the role of annoying older brother.

And then, perhaps he'd play the role of annoying boyfriend, dragging his woman out of there because he missed her after four days and calls and texts weren't even remotely a good replacement.

But he didn't get that far.

Because as he turned on Main Street to drive by her place, he saw her car was in front of Tangled.

The damned woman worked too hard.

So, he'd go in, drag her out, play annoying boyfriend who softened that annoyance by kissing her senseless and promised cinnamon rolls in the morning.

He pulled into the spot next to hers, turned off the ignition, and got out, his eyes drifting to the door.

The *door.*

Fuck.

Moving before he fully processed that the door was shattered, glass glittering on the sidewalk, Chance sprinted for the front of the shop. His hand was in his pocket, pulling out his cell, calling 9-1-1.

The dispatcher picked up.

He rattled off the situation as he pushed through the door, and then hung up, pulled out his gun, ignoring the woman's orders to stay outside and that someone had called it in already and police were on the way.

Mist didn't have an alarm.

No one was around.

If the police were coming, that meant Mist had been scared enough to call 9-1-1—or fuck, he hoped she was okay enough to call because he knew she was smart enough to do it if she wasn't hurt or—

Cutting that line of thought off, he moved.

He wasn't waiting. He'd proceed cautiously, silently, but not fucking slowly. Not when Misty was in danger. Not a fucking a chance.

He stepped through the glass on the concrete and littering the nice hardwood floor inside, wincing at the noise. His gaze flicked around the space. The large table where she held her classes was empty and untouched, along with all the wicker baskets on the shelves. Her register and the glass case beneath it were obliterated, computer parts everywhere, pieces of the drawers and case scattered.

No sign of anyone, however.

There was a noise in the storeroom, and he immediately shifted that way, gun raised, moving through the shadows, trying to get a glimpse of what was happening.

He got that glimpse.

And then promptly lost his shit.

Or at least, he lost cautious and silent.

Chance slammed through the door, already half-hanging off its hinges, a wooden chair tossed to one side, its back cracked, one leg missing. There were enough boxes scattered everywhere to tell him that Misty had been scared enough—and smart enough—to try and barricade herself in after she'd called the police.

Those details he'd noted on a cursory glance as he barreled through the debris, moving across the room with rage boiling beneath his skin.

That was enough for him.

Because Misty was cowering in the corner, blood pouring down her face.

She was conscious, breathing. She was also fucking terrified, one arm above her head, as though to fend off another blow, her other held close to her body and at an odd angle.

"Open it!" the man screamed, raising the bat.

"Drop it," Chance barked, drawing the man's focus, not willing to risk taking the time to get close enough to disarm the fucker, not when it might mean the man might get another opportunity to take that bat to Misty.

The man growled, stepped toward Chance, and thankfully away from Misty.

"Drop the fucking bat," Chance ordered, keeping his gun raised as he moved closer, as he tried to keep the man's attention, tried to make sure he wouldn't swing at Misty again because Chance couldn't get between them, was too far away to deflect the bat if the intruder tried to hit her again.

"Fuck you," the man snapped.

His eyes were wild.

His eyes were glassy.

His eyes were *desperate*.

Fuck.

The man was going to do something stupid.

And not even a heartbeat after that, the man *did* do something stupid.

He swung the bat down. Swung it toward Misty.

Chance fired. Once. He didn't aim for the leg or arm. He aimed for the torso. He aimed to take the man down. He aimed…to kill. Because this wasn't a fucking movie. His woman was bleeding and huddled in the corner, a man who'd already hurt her between them and swinging a bat. She was terrified out of her mind, and this lunatic was responsible for it, wasn't backing down, was trying to hurt her again.

So, he did his best to eliminate that threat.

The man dropped.

Chance kicked the bat away, holstered his weapon, and turned to face Misty. She was pale, so fucking pale, and her hair was stained bright red, so *fucking* bright. He moved to take her in his arms, but she skittered back from him, cramming herself back even further into the wall, trying to disappear between the desk and the boxes.

Fuck.

He crouched, extended a hand slowly toward her. "It's me, Cloudless." She was in a ball, trembling, her stare not seeming to process him. "You're okay now. I've got you."

She shook her head.

He kept an eye on the man behind them. Alive and groaning. Bleeding on Misty's floor.

"Fuck," he whispered.

Sirens sounded.

Loud and close.

"I'm going to touch you, Cloudless. It's me. It's Chance." Slowly, he reached for her, lightly resting his hand on her foot. She jumped. "It's okay. It's Chance. I'm here. You're safe."

Finally, she blinked. "Chance?"

"Yeah, baby."

Her eyes filled with tears, and she launched out of the corner, throwing her arms around him. Or at least *one* arm. The other she immediately dropped to her chest.

"Careful," he said, picking her up and angling her away from the man.

He heard boots in the front room, voices calling out, "Police."

"In here," he called back. "We need an ambulance!"

Not that he gave a fuck if the asshole who was groaning and bleeding on the floor died, but Misty didn't need that happening in her shop, and she needed someone to look at her injuries.

Two officers came through the space, guns drawn, flashlights on, blinding him, fucking with his night vision.

"Intruder is down, needs medical attention," he called.

One officer nodded, moved toward the man.

The other flicked on the lights to the storeroom, causing them all to blink again, and then made the call for additional responders on his radio.

"Misty is hurt, needs it, too," Chance said. "My gun is in my holster at my right hip. I'm Chance Jackson. Licensed P.I. Misty's boyfriend. ID in my back pocket."

The officer who'd flicked on the light came forward and removed Chance's wallet, took his gun. "Don't move," he ordered, staring at Chance's ID. "What happened?"

"I saw her car out front. Then the broken door. Came back here, saw the intruder with a bat over her. Tried to get him to back down, but he went to hit her again. I fired once when he tried to hurt her again, and he went down. Wound in the upper torso."

A nod.

The tension the officers had been holding since they'd rushed the storeroom dissipating slightly.

"I'm going to run your ID."

Misty was shuddering in his arms and too damned pale as she clung to him. "Fine. But I'm taking her outside," he told them.

"Don't go far."

Chance nodded then added, "Ambulance doesn't get here in the next few minutes, I'm driving her to the hospital."

That got him a nod in return.

Then he was moving, blinking as he went back into the dark,

navigating through the glass and shattered register pieces and taking Misty to his SUV. He opened the door, sat her on the passenger's seat then started to tug her arm away from where it was still holding tight, intending to retrieve a blanket from the trunk.

But when he tried to pull her free, she panicked.

"No!"

"I'm not going anywhere, baby," he murmured, trying to stroke a hand down her hair then immediately stopping upon finding it matted with blood. His temper flared, and he wanted to go back inside and shoot the fucker again. The only thing that was stopping him was the fact that Misty needed him. "I'm just going to grab you a blanket. You're shaking."

"No!" she cried again, clinging to him with one arm, reaching with the other and then jerking it back again, a sound of pain that made his temper rage again.

It took everything in him to rein it in.

He gritted his teeth, jaw clenching so tight it felt like the bones would crack.

Then, instead of arguing with her, he just swept her into his arms again, carried her to the back of his SUV, and hit the button to open the tailgate. He sat there with her in his lap, sliding his arm around her waist, using his other to grab a blanket, fumbling to wrap it around her.

By the time he got her covered, another cruiser had pulled up, an ambulance on its heels.

The paramedics ran inside, pushing a stretcher as they went, bags loaded on top.

Misty was still shivering, her face in his neck, her breaths shuddering.

He knew she needed to be checked out, needed a doctor or a paramedic or a trip to the ER. But he didn't think anything was critical and knew that even more than getting that treatment, she needed to be held, to be made to feel safe.

Another ambulance would come.

She'd be on it.

Or he'd drive her to the hospital himself.

But right now, she needed comfort and gentle, needed him to keep the demons at bay.

At least for a few minutes.

17

PURPLE

Misty

THE SMALL PENLIGHT flashed on one eye and then the other, making her wince and blink.

But apparently the doctor was satisfied.

She put the penlight away, stashing it in the pocket of her lab coat, and moved to the computer, typing notes into her chart.

Dr. Montergo.

Misty had seen her around town.

She'd even had a conversation with her at last year's Holiday Tree Lighting ceremony. Raven Montergo. Unusual name, but totally fitting for the beautiful woman. Unusual brown eyes, almost like topaz, but with a hint of mahogany. Hair the color of coffee—sans milk or cream—a deep, dark russet that was almost black and completely straight. It shone like something from a shampoo commercial and paired with her body—tall and slender—she appeared as graceful as a ballerina.

Striking. Unique.

But her personality was all small-town.

Warm and welcoming, totally down to gossip, and ready to join the Bake Sale Brigade, or the football team's Booster Club, or to hang lights for that Holiday Tree Lighting ceremony (how they'd met).

That personality had completely morphed the moment she'd laid eyes on Misty.

Then fury had made those unusual eyes spark with fire; her face had gone hard. She'd quietly, but firmly—and Misty meant *firmly*—had ordered Chance from the room. Chance, who'd held her after he'd shot a man for her. Chance, who hadn't blinked at her freak-out, her panic when he stepped away, nor at her irrational fear of him leaving. Chance, who'd carried her to the back of his SUV and held her so gently, held her until she'd stopped shaking, until the fear had subsided and the pain had risen. Who'd seemed to understand that and had told the police who'd shown up while she'd been terrified out of her mind that they could get her statement in the morning after she'd gotten checked out and some rest.

Chance had begun to argue about leaving, but Raven Montergo, *Dr.* Montergo, had fixed him with a look that had him cutting off his retort, gently brushing his knuckles over Misty's cheek, and saying he would be right outside.

Now silence fell as Dr. Montergo typed.

Then she moved slowly to the exam table, perching on the edge, reaching out for the splint on Misty's right arm. "Ortho will be in shortly to cast this. The break isn't bad, but you might be out of knitting commission for six to eight weeks."

Misty nodded.

She knew it was broken, had felt the bones snap when she'd managed to get the arm over her head and between her skull and the bat. She hadn't managed to block the bat altogether. It had still hit her head, her temple, hard enough that she'd gone out for a few seconds, and now had a half dozen staples in her scalp, along with a line of stitches at her hairline.

When Misty had come to after the world had gone fuzzy for a few moments, it was to find the man shaking her hard enough to rattle her teeth. He'd screamed about the safe when he'd seen her eyes fly open, then he had lifted the bat again—

She shuddered.

Dr. Montergo didn't miss it.

"You're safe," she murmured.

Misty sucked in a breath, released it slowly, nodded. "I know." Another breath. "And I know why you sent Chance out. The intruder didn't rape me, didn't touch me aside from with the bat." A wince. "He just wanted me to open the safe. He wanted the money. Not—not me." Her lips trembled, and she pressed them flat.

At that point, Raven made an appearance, the doctor persona sliding away as she smiled encouragingly, her voice still gentle, but the fierce that had sent Chance into the hall had been banked. "You did good, sweetheart," Raven murmured. "You protected your head. Because of that, you don't have a concussion, lucky for you."

"Thanks," Misty whispered. "Though not too lucky since I ended up with a broken arm," she muttered.

"Better a broken arm than a broken brain."

That was true.

Raven patted her leg. "I'm going to write you a prescription for pain meds and sleeping pills. I want you to take them tonight."

"I—"

"Just tonight." And now Dr. Montergo was back. "Tomorrow on, you can decide what you need. But tonight, sleep with your man, let him hold you and feel safe, and allow your body to get the rest it needs to recover."

"I—" Her protest was on the tip of her tongue, but then she swallowed it down. Because Dr. Montergo was back. Because even if she wasn't, what Raven was saying was right.

She was exhausted.

She was hurting.

She needed rest...and she needed Chance.

Raven or Dr. Montergo or whoever the woman in the room with her was seemed to understand that. She patted Misty's leg again and stood. "I'll go get Chance. We'll get your discharge paperwork going so that as soon as ortho is done, you'll be able to go home."

"Thanks," Misty murmured.

"I'd say anytime," Raven said, "but I don't want to see you in my ER again."

Misty smiled. Somehow, despite what had happened, her lips had curved up and she was smiling. "I can't say I want to be back." An awkward chuckle slipped out and she winced. "Not that you guys haven't been nice. It's just—"

Dr. Montergo laughed as she stood and moved to the computer again, tugging the rolling cart toward her and typing again. "You don't want to be back. Trust me, I get it. No hard feelings." A beat. "Plus, I think I was the one banning you from my department in the first place."

That was true.

"Right," Misty said and processed that the pain killers must have finally started working, because she was getting a pleasant, floating feeling, like she was buzzed. "Well, I think the only reason I'll come back of my own volition is bringing you guys double fudge cupcakes to thank you for taking care of me."

Raven was back, smiling sweetly. "Now, *that* I could get behind."

"It's a deal."

There was a knock at the door. Dr. Montergo told them to come in, and Misty turned to see a younger blond woman in maroon scrubs roll in a cart. "Misty, this is Lavender. She's the best ortho tech around. She'll get you casted and comfortable, and I'll work on those discharge papers. Lav," she went on, pushing in the keyboard tray and heading for the exit, "this is Misty. You take care of her really well, and she'll bring us the best double fudge chocolate cupcakes as payment." A smile. "Trust me. You want the cupcakes."

The blonde nodded, her mouth turned up to reveal two dimples. "Not that I wouldn't take care of you, but double fudge cupcakes sound awesome."

Dr. Montergo clapped Lav on the shoulder. "That is the correct answer." She met Misty's eyes. "I'll tell Chance he can come back in?"

Its inflection was a question because…it was a question.

Misty nodded.

Raven inclined her head, slipped out the door.

Lav had barely gotten her cart pushed to the bedside before Chance had returned to the room, moving around the ortho tech, and coming to grab Misty's uninjured hand. His hair was askew, as though he'd been constantly running his hands through it. He looked like he'd aged a hundred years, deep lines around his mouth, his eyes, stubble on his jaw. "You okay?" he asked softly.

"I'm great!" she replied.

And she was. That floating feeling had expanded. There was no more pain. Raven had said she'd done good. Chance was there. She was safe. She wasn't hurting.

"Do you want white, blue, purple, or pink?" Lavender asked.

"Purple," Chance murmured, when Misty's brows dragged together. "She wants purple. It's her favorite color."

Lavender glanced at Misty. "Purple?" she asked, apparently looking for confirmation.

Misty, meanwhile, had helium in her veins; she was in the sky, drifting among the clouds, swimming through the blue dome, free-styling or maybe breast-stroking or perhaps butter-flying. No. Back-stroking. Definitely she'd be doing a back-stroke if she could swim through the clouds. That was the only stroke she'd been any good at on the swim team.

Meaning that one time she'd gotten an eighth place ribbon.

Her best ever finishing. *Ever.*

Repeated for emphasis.

Because while Rob had killed it on the Minnows—Stoneybrook's youth swimming team—she'd mostly liked figuring out the different ways to braid her hair to stash it under her swim cap and the thick, fluffy parkas.

And goggles.

She'd liked matching them to her cap, to her suit.

It was great fun.

But she hadn't exactly been skilled.

"Misty?"

The tone of Chance's voice made it clear that it wasn't the first time he'd said her name.

"Yeah?" she asked, blinking up at him.

"Purple for your cast, baby?"

A nod. "Purple is my favorite color."

He cupped her cheek, running his thumb along her jaw. "I know, Cloudless." His eyes drifted away. "Purple," he said again, and Misty realized distantly he was talking to Lavender, when the other woman said, "Got it," and gently began to shift Misty's arm, removing the splint and positioning her wrist in a way that didn't feel great. It hurt like hell, actually, cutting through that pleasant fog, as though the strings holding her to that helium balloon that had sent her flying had been cut and she was falling back toward Earth.

And continued to descend as Lavender began casting her.

First, Lav slipped a sock sort of thing over Misty's arm, tugging it up above her elbow and cutting it with a pair of odd-looking scissors so that it barely covered her fingertips. Then Lav used the same scissors to make a hole for Misty's thumb.

That felt fine.

That didn't hurt.

The positioning did.

As did the casting. It wasn't the worst type of pain, just a persistent throb and an occasional jab. But it wasn't comfortable, even though her pain meds were trying to send her floating. They eventually wore off.

No buzz.

No sky.

Just reality.

And trying not to think about what had happened.

The shattering glass. The baseball bat meeting the register, the case, her arm. The man's face, gathered in a frightening mask. His voice, unhinged and loud and terrifying, ringing in her ears.

Warm fingers covered those of her uninjured hand as Chance shifted closer, somehow seeming to understand that she'd taken a mental turn and was able to read what was spiraling through her mind. "You're okay?" he asked softly.

She nodded, not feeling okay in the least, but also understanding that there was nothing to be done about it.

She wanted her bed and Chance. She wanted to sleep and pretend this hadn't happened.

"Cloudless," he murmured, his lips to her ear. "*Honey.*"

"Please, stop asking if I'm okay," she whispered. "I'm not, but I want to pretend I am."

He straightened, and Misty bit back a wince when the fiberglass material Lavender was wrapping on her wrist went tight and hot.

Chance's stare was on hers, holding it, staring deep into her eyes. Then he nodded.

"Tonight, you can pretend." A squeeze of his fingers. "I've got you, baby."

Just words.

But they took that boulder that was sitting on her chest and hefted it away, rolled it down some hill, allowing it to land somewhere in the distance, somewhere she wouldn't have to deal with it until tomorrow, or the next day.

He kissed her temple.

He held her hand.

And when the cast was done, when she was discharged, he bundled her into his SUV and drove her home.

It was exactly what she needed.

18

SISTERS

Chance

"I NEED to get someone to cover up the front door," she whispered.

They were almost back to Misty's place, and it was the first time she'd spoken since the hospital room, since she'd asked him to help her pretend.

"I've got it covered," he told her. "I called Rob." He touched her cheek lightly when she whirled in her seat and frowned at him. "I know you didn't want to bother him, but if it was my sister, I'd want to know."

Quiet.

He kept talking. "Rob went by the shop to get everything secure." And to clean up, not that Chance was going to tell her that.

She didn't need to be thinking about her blood staining the floor, or the fact that there was glass everywhere, or that her point-of-sale system had been reduced to thousands of pieces.

It was bad enough that her jaw clenched and the silence descended again, this time heavier when he mentioned her brother. Reality was intruding, and she wanted to pretend, so he quickly got the rest of it over with. "He's going to go back to his place after it's taken care of and will call me in the morning." Chance squeezed her hand, relieved when her fingers tightened around his in return. "I don't think I can put him off much further past that. I'm sure he'll be over at first light, even if I tell him you want more space."

Her nose wrinkled.

Her shoulders rose and fell on a breath.

"I don't think I actually want space." She bit her lip. "I know I told you not to call him, but…"

He waited, and when she didn't go on, Chance asked, "You want me to tell him to come to your place when he's done?" Another squeeze of that unbroken hand. "I'm sure he'd be relieved to be able to see you."

She went still, her teeth pressing into her bottom lip. "N-no," she whispered, shaking her head, giving him a glimpse of the bandage on her right temple. "He just got back from vacation, and Soph is pregnant. They must be tired." Her shoulders slumped. "Plus, if she stays home, I don't want him to have to stay away from Soph any longer than he is already. They have too much time apart as it is."

He pulled into her driveway, not about to argue with her, but after he'd parked, he thumbed off a quick text to Rob. She might not want to bother him, but Misty wanted her brother there, and Rob was desperate to come check on his sister, Soph in the same boat. Chance's sister had wanted to come to the hospital immediately, and it was only his strong encouragement to get Tangled back into some semblance of shape for Misty that had convinced her and Rob to not come to the waiting room.

Rob had called him after the doctor had kicked Chance out of the room, and he knew that Misty's brother had been into the shop, had seen the glass and damaged counter and the blood in the storeroom when Rob had whispered simply, "I'm going to kill him."

"I tried that," Chance muttered. "Fucker didn't die."

Rob was quiet. "She's lucky you were there."

It was Chance's turn to grow quiet. "Would have been luckier if I'd gotten there earlier."

Chance knew that shit happened, that bad people did bad things and sometimes swept up good people along with them, but fuck, if he wasn't kicking himself for not calling, for not texting. If he had, she might have been home waiting for him, instead of easy pickings for a robber at the store.

His cell buzzed, Rob saying he'd be there in five minutes.

He texted back, said he was still going to lock the door behind him and to knock when he got there.

To which Rob replied:

We have a key.

Good.

Misty had started to open her door by the time he made it around to her, what with the texting and him pausing to grab the bag of bloodied clothes the nurses had bagged for her, so he carefully tugged it a little wider, made sure her belt was unbuckled—it was—and then carefully scooped her up into his arms. She shivered, probably chilled in the thin scrubs the hospital had given her, and he hurried to the front door, not realizing until he got there that neither of them had a way to unlock it. Her purse was in her shop, and he hadn't been able to grab it before they headed to the hospital since the officers were processing the scene.

Misty seemed to pick up on their predicament and process that fact much more quickly than he did. "Hide-a-key," she said, lifting her uninjured arm and pointing to a rock by the bottom step.

"Got it," he murmured, setting her gently on the bench by the door and going to the rock, flipping it over, and finding the hidden compartment. A flick to get it open, another to close it.

Then the rock was back in place, and he was unlocking the door.

Misty moved like she was going to walk inside, but he beat her to it, picking her up and carrying her to the couch.

He'd barely got her settled when there was the scrape of a key in the door he'd locked—two minutes or two hours, he wasn't taking the smallest chance with her.

Rob came in first, Soph behind him.

He heard his sister gasp, her breath hitching, and a sob traversing the sound waves of the room. Catching her eye, he sharply shook his head, silently telling her to hold it together. Yeah, she was emotional because of the pregnancy, but Misty didn't need someone crying over her. She needed calm and caring and strong shoulders to lean on.

Luckily, Soph interpreted his look, sucked in a breath, and got it together.

"I'll get you some pajamas," she said, turning for the hall, though he didn't miss her dashing away her tears as she did so. "Do you want a bath, Mist? With your special oil?"

His girl liked baths?

He filed that away for later. He'd buy her a fucking vat of that special oil if it meant she repeated what she did when Soph suggested the bath—her shoulders relaxing, the deep V between her brows evening out, her voice soft when she replied, "Yes, that would be amazing. Thanks."

Soph nodded, disappeared down the hall, and a moment later, they heard the water turn on, drawers opening and closing in the bedroom.

Rob was frozen, standing in the hall, his hands fisted at his sides.

And Chance understood why.

Misty's hair was still stained crimson with blood, her face was bruising, her eye swollen and already blackening. The purple cast stood out sharply against her pale skin—he made a mental note to pick up a cast cover from the drug store the next day—but he knew the moment that Rob processed the color.

His face smoothed out. His hands relaxed.

Chance watched him visibly bank that fury.

He walked over, slowing when he got close.

Misty stood up and walked into his arms, and he held her like she was the most delicate glass, his head dropping as he whispered something in her ear.

She burrowed deeper, holding him tighter.

Only then did Chance move away from Misty and give Rob the space to comfort his sister. He went through her kitchen and found a bag he could secure around her cast temporarily, then went into the bathroom to comfort *his* sister.

Her eyes were red and a little swollen, but she wasn't actively crying any longer.

The moment he crossed over the threshold, she launched herself at him and lost it again, her tears soaking his shirt.

He let her have that, stroked her back. Yes, it was pregnancy hormone related. But also, yes, it was her finding and falling in love with Rob related. She'd been too closed down due to the shit her bio parents had heaped on her to connect with anyone for far too long. Well, she was wide open now. She was feeling everything, and while he didn't want her to lose her shit in front of Misty, he wasn't going to chastise her for losing it with him in private.

"She's okay," he said, stroking a hand down her spine. "She'll be okay."

Soph lifted her head, met his eyes. "Of course, she will."

Then she burrowed deeper into him and kept crying.

He held tight and let her.

19

MUFFINS

Misty

IT HAD BEEN two days since the robbery, since the baseball bat, and though the whole of Stoneybrook had given her space yesterday, mostly because it had been really late by the time Chance had brought her home from the hospital the night before, and mostly because she'd slept the day away (thus, she hadn't been aware if anyone had come to visit or bring casseroles or just lay eyes on her), the denizens of Stoneybrook had decided Misty had been given enough space.

Case in point, that morning Frankie and Maggie had descended, Soph and Rob had redescended—they'd both stayed for a while after she'd lost her shit in Rob's arms, after her brother had carried her to bed and held her tight in a way he hadn't done since their parents had died. Eventually, she'd gotten it together and ordered him to take Soph home so she could rest.

They'd fought her, but Chance had stepped in.

He'd bustled them out.

But not before she'd met Soph's eyes, taken her hand—a hand that had been holding Misty's or bringing tissues or running her a bath she didn't get around to taking because by the time she got her shit together to kick them out, the water had grown cold—and said, "You'll be a good mom, Soph."

Soph's eyes had filled with tears, but she'd simply sniffed, nodded, and kissed Misty's cheek.

Then they'd gone.

Then Chance had added more hot water to the bath, sat with her while she was in it, a plastic bag wrapped around her cast, so she could doze and pretend that a man who'd clearly been disturbed or on drugs or…whatever, had not taken a bat to her in order to get a couple hundred dollars in petty cash. And when she was done, he'd blown out the candles, hit the plug on the tub, and hefted her out before the water was fully gone, even though that had meant she'd gotten him all wet. She'd protested. He'd said he didn't want her to get cold.

And if she'd been retaining any pieces of her heart, holding anything back, at that point it was a lost cause.

Her heart was Chance's.

After wrapping her in a towel, he'd set her on the bed, slipped off the plastic bag, made sure every inch of her was dry, and then he'd tucked her under the covers, gone to her drawers, pulled out her pajamas, and had carefully helped her get dressed.

Her eyes had been drooping then, but he'd given her a sleeping pill and some pain medicine anyway.

Then he'd climbed into bed next to her, wrapped her in his arms, and had murmured, "You're safe. I'm here."

That drooping had transformed into *out*.

And when she'd woken the next day, her bed had been empty, it was almost dinner time, and Chance had been in her kitchen, making some sort of pasta sauce that was so garlicky it almost burned her nose.

In other words, it had turned out to be fucking delicious.

Turning as she stumbled into the kitchen, her body hurting and drool, no doubt, crusting on her face, joining right along with sheet creases and flushed cheeks, he'd smiled and said, "Hey, beautiful."

The way he'd said it had told her he meant it.

The way he'd said it had erased the niggling of fear that he might look at her differently in the light of the morning—or early evening, as it was. Not that he *would* look at her differently. She just…well, she *felt* different. A little busted up. A little vulnerable. A little…suffice to say, the man in her shop with the baseball bat had shattered her careful picture of the world.

She'd known that bad things happened, that the world wasn't all rosy.

It was just—outside of her parents dying—none of that bad had touched her.

Chance had stirred the pot, turned down the heat on the stovetop, and then he'd left the sauce to simmer, taking her uninjured hand and leading her to the bathroom. Gentle touches, a soft kiss to her temple. Her toothbrush ready with toothpaste. The shower on. A cover he must have picked up at some point during the day placed over her cast. Him stripping down and stepping into the stream, helping her in, washing her hair with a towel covering her stitches so they didn't get wet, soaping her body up and rinsing it gently, even though she saw his jaw clenching when he took in the bruises that had arisen on her skin since the night before.

He'd taken care of her in a way she had never been taken care of. And her brother was no slouch in the taking care of department, considering he'd shown up that night, had held her while she'd cried, had fixed the door to the shop, cleaned it up, got her a new point of sale system, and had glass for new register stand on order.

But Chance had a hand in that, too.

Rob told him he'd called and texted, keeping her brother in the loop, like when she'd been rethinking keeping Rob away so he wouldn't be inconvenienced.

Which had earned her a scolding—albeit a gentle one—

when Rob and Soph had turned up that morning with cinnamon rolls and coffees, Rob reiterating that she was his sister and as thus never an inconvenience and doing it by saying some really nice things ("You've grown into an incredible woman, Dewdrop, and I know you like to do things on your own, but you could never be an inconvenience," and, "I love you, sweetheart, and I'm so sorry this happened," and "I'm getting the shop back up to snuff and building you a new case for your register, and you can just suck it up and accept it.") And maybe the last part of that statement wasn't exactly nice—orders rarely were—but it was still Rob and her brother being there for her and caring for her and the undertones of it were nice.

And Chance had orchestrated it, made sure Rob was there, prioritized the shop, held her while she slept, washed her hair, cooked for her. He'd even worked with Rob to figure out how to place the order for materials she'd just finished inventorying when everything had gone to shit.

She hadn't thought that was something she ever wanted, hadn't thought she'd be able to relax with someone taking care of her, hadn't thought she needed it.

She'd always handled her own stuff.

But she couldn't deny having Chance help her shoulder all of that, looking after her, felt wonderful and—

"Eat that," Mrs. Hutchinson demanded, dropping a plate in front of her.

Misty blinked out of her reverie, happy to be in her shop, though not all that pleased to be in it with Mrs. Hutchinson. "Thank you very much for making it, but I'm not hungry. I—"

Mrs. Hutchinson shoved the plate with a bran muffin—yes, a fucking *bran* muffin—toward her. "*Eat,*" she ordered.

Gritting her teeth, Misty picked up the muffin and took a huge bite.

And then promptly felt like her jaw had been welded

together. "Mmm," she said, forcing out the sound while trying not to gag because *God*, that was foul.

Eventually, she managed to get the bite down, nearly draining her mug of coffee in the process.

By then, Mrs. Hutchinson had moved to the displays of yarn —thank God for the prospect of new and shiny projects and their ability to distract bossy old ladies from making sure she finished that hell of a muffin.

Soph sidled up next to her, and without one word, the muffin disappeared, the wrapper staying as evidence of her "eating" it, and then her sister-in-law was gone, slipping into the storeroom.

Misty did not miss the soft *thunk* of the muffin hitting the trash can she kept back there. She smiled at Soph when she returned, acknowledging her assistance in Muffin Gate, and receiving a wink in return.

"Where should we put this blend?" Frankie asked, wisely not commenting on the bran muffin disappearing, as she held up a skein of lovely pale green yarn.

Okay, Misty thought that *all* yarn was lovely.

But this one was especially so. Mainly because that soft green reminded her of the streaks in Chance's eyes, and since she'd been mentally mooning over him and all that caretaking and lovely niceness, the yarn reminding her of his eyes then reminded her of his face—all strong lines and dark stubble, yum—which then reminded her of his body—muscular, but not over the top, taller than her, harder than hers, and a chest that had just the right amount of hair (meaning that he wasn't Chewbacca, but he definitely felt like a man, also yum).

And so, she was thinking of Chance's body and not the yarn, and apparently doing it for some time because she barely heard Maggie pause her perusal of the box she was supposed to be sorting—rhinestone-covered knitting needles, which was no surprise since Maggie and sparkles went hand in hand. She certainly wasn't aware of Chance coming up to her, not until his arm slid around her shoulders and kissed her uninjured temple.

God, she liked when he did that.

"Whatcha thinking, Cloudless?" he murmured in her ear.

She shifted, caught a glimpse of those green eyes with the seafoam streaks that had jump-started her fantasizing, caught that they held enough mischief to tell her he had a good idea, and decided to just give it to him. "You. And all that you've done for me the past couple of days, not to mention that you saved me from getting hit with a bat and shot a man to protect me." That mischief faded, and she stepped closer, pressing her front to his. "But more than thinking about how wonderful you've been—which you've *definitely* been and all that wonderful has made me fall completely, head over heels in love with you, and not in a weird hero-worship kind of way because you saved me and took care of me the last couple of days, but because I liked you a lot before, and in this shitty situation you showed me the kind of man you are—which, in case you're wondering is a fucking good one—and all of this is to say, I was thinking that and then the yarn reminded me of your eyes and the little pale green streaks in your irises, and that got me thinking about your body which got me thinking about how much I like it naked and against me, not to mention your cock inside me, and—"

"Cloudless."

The sharp bite of his voice had her blinking and jarring right out of her rambling.

His palm cupped her cheek, fingers brushing the bottom of the bandage on her temple. "First," he said, his voice still gruff, and that might have hurt if not for the wealth of emotions in his eyes and the next words he said, "I love you, too. Hands down. With all my heart. I've never met a woman like you. Never met *anyone* who made me *know—know,* not think—that I had to take the risk of having someone I loved at home, someone who might leave me or I might leave them, and we might end up in pieces because of it. But that I'll gladly take the risk because knowing that I get you in my life in any way, for any amount of time makes that risk completely worth it."

Misty's eyes stung.

A tear escaped.

He scooped it off her bottom lashes.

"What's second?" she breathed, after taking a moment to hold those words close and knowing that she would never forget them, not for as long as she lived.

"Mmm?"

His fingers were moving on her skin, light touches on her cheek, her jaw, her neck.

"You said *first*," she whispered, tilting her head so he could trace those rough digits over her collarbone. Sensitive. So fucking sensitive. "So," she said, shivering, "what's second?"

He froze.

Then grinned. But she only saw that smirk for a second before he bent his head and whispered in her ear. "Second," he murmured, making her shiver again, even more fiercely this time, "I was going to remind you we have an audience."

She gasped, turned her head, saw that Maggie and Frankie were listening unabashedly, right along with Mrs. Hutchinson, Rob, Soph, and several of her customers.

Chance kept whispering. "So, I didn't think you wanted to be talking about my cock inside you."

Her cheeks flooded with heat.

His lips found her earlobe, nipped lightly. "So, you love me?"

That heat didn't go away, but she didn't shy away from him, just shifted so she could meet his gaze, so his mouth was close to hers. "I love you." Her lips dropped to his and because she'd only ever given him straight, could only continue giving him straight in this moment, too, she added, "And I love your cock."

She heard Maggie snicker behind them.

She heard a groan—Rob, she realized when she heard him

say, "Fuck, could have lived my life with not hearing my sister say the word *cock* twice in as many minutes."

Frankie just giggled.

"What was that?" Mrs. Hutchinson all but yelled. "What did she say?"

Soph sniffed.

Frankie murmured, "She said she loves him."

"Hmph." A beat that was long enough for Misty to spin in Chance's arms, to see the collection gathered in front of the makeshift register stand Rob had put together for her. "Good," Mrs. Hutchinson said when Misty's eyes hit hers. "He's a good one."

Then she barreled for the door, pushed it open, pausing as Misty's slightly beat-up—kind of like her, she supposed—bell tinkled to look back at them.

"Eat the rest of the bran muffins," she ordered, nodding to the basket sitting on the makeshift counter Rob had erected, a basket Misty had somehow missed noticing before, much to her horror, seeing as she needed to resurrect Operation Muffin Gate. "They're good for you." A beat. "I'm coming back later with chicken noodle soup and to buy that mauve merino blend. And the pattern for the teddy bear. My granddaughter *needs* that teddy bear."

A heartbeat later, she was gone.

The bell tinkled as the door closed.

Then Soph did her a solid and the rest of the bran muffins hit the trash can.

Thank God for small miracles.

20

MOVING BOXES

Chance

SHOVING the final box into his truck, he turned and shook hands with his landlord.

The man wasn't getting a bad deal. Chance was leaving a month early, even though he'd already paid rent for that month and the one following. Plus, Tony already had someone ready to move into the apartment.

Not a bad deal.

And he wouldn't be missing Chance at all, not when he got double rent.

Not that Chance would be missing him either.

Tony was a nice guy, but the apartment wasn't exactly stellar. It had been a place to live, to crash when he was home. His office had been nicer for obvious reasons. He couldn't have clients walking into a shit-hole.

But his lease on that had been up for several months now, ever since Rob had settled in with Soph and Chance had visited Stoneybrook. He'd known that he was going to move closer, especially when his parents had taken the first step and headed that way, his brothers then following suit.

They were a close family.

He wasn't going to be the one left behind.

But he hadn't settled on Stoneybrook itself until Misty had barreled into his SUV.

Now he knew there was nowhere else he'd rather be.

It had been six weeks since he'd driven by Misty's shop and saw the shattered glass, six weeks since she'd been hurt, six weeks where he'd spent nearly every moment with her.

He'd never believed in utopia, in perfection.

But hell if that wasn't what he'd found with Misty.

Not that it was *all* perfection. They'd fought just the night before. She'd been frustrated by his "hovering" and trying to do everything for her. This had come to a head, namely because she was getting the cast off that day. He'd wanted to put off his trip to go with her, and she'd bluntly refused.

They'd argued.

Then she'd kissed him, and they'd continued the argument while fucking on the couch.

Then she'd given him an orgasm that had made his head explode, or at least that was the reason he was clinging to for giving in and letting her go to her appointment by herself, even though he wanted to hold her hand when the doctor unleashed a scary fucking saw to cut off some fiberglass strapped around her freaking *arm*.

He'd be back late that night, and he'd go to her house, crawl into bed next to her, and kiss all that newly exposed skin.

Bonus was she hadn't asked for the key he'd snagged from the fake rock outside her house a while back.

Not that he'd been planning to return it.

Not that he *would* have given it back.

And no, she couldn't orgasm her way out of that.

Plus, he'd made a copy of it, and restocked the hide-a-key in the days after the assault, so she'd be covered despite his key thieving.

At the moment, though, he turned over the keys to his apartment, closed the tailgate of his SUV, got in the driver's seat, and texted Misty, letting her know he was on his way home.

Then he hit the road.

She called back just as he hit the highway.

"How's the naked wrist?" he asked.

"Weird," she said with a laugh. "How's the full SUV?"

"Full."

She laughed again, and it was as pleasant as that bell tinkling above the door at Tangled. "I missed you," she murmured, giving him that without any games, without any barriers. Just sweet and Misty and telling him that she liked having him around.

"I missed you, too, Cloudless." And he had. And he knew he'd give her what she had given him, without any games, without walls.

He'd never thought he would dive into something like this with her.

Never thought he'd be open to loving a woman in that way.

Never thought he would find someone like Misty who made loving her so fucking easy.

"You know what I did first thing the moment I got that damned cast off?"

"Knit?" he asked, cruising around cars and knowing the miles would fly by fast so long as she was on the phone with him, that they would crawl when they hung up.

She laughed. "No," she said, "but I'm going to get started on that next."

"So, what did you do, Cloudless?"

He could hear the smile in her voice, even though he couldn't see her gorgeous face. "I made you double fudge cupcakes."

His stomach immediately rumbled.

And loud enough that she heard it, apparently, since she began laughing. "I'm guessing you like that, baby?"

"I'd like it better if I was there," he grumbled.

More laughter. "Drive safe, baby," she murmured. "I'll wait up for you."

"You don't have to do that."

"I—"

She broke off, went quiet.

He gave her a minute to get her thoughts together, then one more to continue with that. *Then* when she still didn't speak, he pressed. "You what, Cloudless?"

An inhale and exhale that rattled through the speakers. "I—"

More breaking off.

He held on to his patience, because he had the feeling he knew what was going through her head, and she needed to say it aloud, to get rid of the demon that had been riding her hard, waking her up at night, having her turn in his arms and burrow into his chest.

"I'd stay up anyway," she whispered after another minute. "I'm not comfortable sleeping without you there."

And there it was.

His work hadn't taken him away overnight since the attack, and he hadn't taken any new cases that would, sensing she'd needed him, and taking the time to search for a place to set up shop in Stoneybrook.

That shop was going to be the spot next door to Tangled, not just because it was next door to Misty and that meant he could see her, could keep an eye on her—though no joke, that was a perk—but also because it was the perfect size for what he needed. Two offices in the back, a reception area in the front, a conference room to one side.

An apartment above.

The last of which he wasn't planning on using, because he liked being at Misty's place, but he also thought that it was a bit presumptuous to move his shit from his old apartment to her house without having a conversation about it.

And part of what made the last six weeks amazing was that,

aside from him spending every night at her place and every free moment of every day together, was that they'd slowed down.

They'd gotten to know each other.

They'd eaten out and gone to the movies (where she'd stolen his popcorn, even though she'd said she hadn't wanted any—so lesson learned, he'd gotten an extra-large the next time they'd hit the theaters). They'd cooked dinner together. They'd gone to Rob and Soph's. She'd endured another big Jackson family get together—this time without any dating pronouncements being hurled across the table, though who knew what would happen at the next big Jackson family get together that would be happening that weekend, since his mom and dad were hosting a backyard barbecue for what seemed like was going to be half of Stoneybrook in attendance.

"That's normal, sweetheart," he said, careful to keep his tone gentle. "What happened to you was traumatic."

"He's out of the hospital."

Chance's stomach immediately soured. "What?"

The gunshot wound had been serious, but the recovery of one Todd Hanover had been complicated by a persistent infection. It had been touch-and-go for a while, and that was all the information the detectives on the case would give him.

Maybe it made Chance a bad person because he'd been hoping the persistent infection would take down fucking Todd Hanover, so Misty didn't have to deal with him potentially being out in the world, after however much time the fucker served, haunting her actions, fueling her nightmares, making her feel unsafe in a place that was supposed to be hers.

"Detective Hopkins called me this morning," she went on. "He's going to get booked tonight, and he could potentially bail out by the morning."

Fuck.

Fuck.

His fingers clenched on the steering wheel. "I'm going to ask Carter to come stay until I get there."

"Oh, Chance, that's not—"

"And Frankie and Maggie," he added, talking over her bull-shit protest, because it was just that.

Bullshit.

Frankie and Maggie were goofy, but they were good friends. They'd spent a lot of time with Misty and had taken turns helping her man Tangled until she'd gotten back on her feet and could manage most everything—except for some classes Frankie taught in Misty's place—on her own.

"And—"

"Don't you dare call my brother," she snapped. "Soph and Rob are at their twenty-week ultrasound, and then Rob is taking her out to dinner. They deserve a nice night out."

That was true.

"I won't call Rob and Soph," he agreed.

"Or the others."

"You're not here to orgasm me into submission with that sexy body of yours. I'm calling Carter. You call your girlfriends. Enjoy a night together without having to worry about that fucker, because Carter will have your back." He kept going. "Watch terrible TV together, paint your nails, knit something, drink champagne to celebrate the cast being gone," he told her. "But don't give that fucker another moment of your time, okay, Cloudless?"

Silence.

Then, "I love you."

He took a breath. "You are so worth it, baby. So *fucking* worth it."

Her breathing hitched. "Chance."

It was a wail.

And that was perfect, too. Because his girl was a crier, and she especially cried when he said nice shit. What was *im*perfect was that he wasn't there to wipe her tears away. But he loved that she felt so deeply and loved that she felt deeply about the things he said.

It made him want to say them more often.

Though just maybe when he was there.

"You're too fucking sweet," she snapped, her breaths shaky, her words punctuated by sniffles. "And you're lucky I love you, even though you make me cry *all the time.*"

He laughed. "Baby, you cry all the time with or without me saying nice things. And I like saying nice things to you. You deserve them. You've made my life better, forgave me even though I nearly fucked things up after our first date—"

"Chance."

"So, I'm going to keep saying them. And you'll keep crying, Cloudless. And we'll keep being perfect together."

Her breathing went shaky again. "I'm not perfect."

"I know," he said. "But you're perfect for me."

A sniffle and then…

More tears.

But eventually he talked her through them, and when she was done crying, he stifled the nice and sweet, confirmed she was going to call her friends. They talked about other shit— some new crochet hooks she'd ordered (and because of the last six weeks, he actually knew what a crochet hook was), how Rob and Soph had gotten caught by little Rylie as they'd tried to sneak off from the picnic they'd all gone to the previous weekend, her plans to fill the new built-in register case Rob had built for her.

By the time they said goodbye and hung up, he had her laughing instead of crying and excited about all the wares she was going to display in that case.

Fuck, he couldn't wait to get home and taste that excitement on his tongue.

21

NEIGHBORS

Misty

"WHAT DO YOU THINK, Sexy Carter Jackson?" Maggie asked, the martini glass in her hand flying around.

Maggie was a gesticulator.

Maggie was also slightly sloshed.

But that slightly sloshed—making her pretty, cream-colored skin come alive with a flush on her high cheekbones, her lush lips turn rosy—meant the glass was nearly empty so none of the cosmo they'd mixed up earlier *sloshed* over the rim.

"And *that's* enough for you," Raven said, Dr. Montergo having firmly been put to pasture for the evening, snagging the glass. Raven drank two cosmos but had cut herself off about an hour earlier, saying she went on call at midnight, so she needed to be sober.

So, Dr. Montergo was less firmly in the pasture and more waiting on the front porch while Raven came out to play.

But Misty was glad she'd come at all.

Raven was funny and good company and could take all the teasing Misty and her friends dished out regularly, could dish it back just as easily. Definitely, it had been the right idea to get on the

Stoneybrook phone tree and get Raven's number. She'd fit in so well that there was no way that she wasn't getting a second invite, whether or not she wanted one. Because Raven had become one of them right about the time she'd walked in with a bottle of vodka, two bags of tortilla chips, and a vat of guacamole from *El Cerrito*.

Now she deftly set the purloined glass on the table, shoved the chips and guac to Maggie, and ordered her to "Eat."

Mags made a face, but she didn't argue, just started shoving chips and guac down her throat. "Well," she said between bites, "you didn't answer, Mr. Sexy Pants Carter Jackson"—Carter pressed his lips flat, probably hoping that Maggie had been thoroughly distracted from her needing a "man's opinion" and he'd be let off the hook—"do you think I should have lied and told him he was a good fuck?"

Frankie's cheeks went pink, and she put her own glass down. "I'll just get some water."

Then she was gone.

Raven stood, followed her into the kitchen. "Water seems like a good idea."

Maggie was undeterred, her slightly glassy eyes glued to Carter. "Should I have lied?" she asked again.

"Mags," Misty began. "That's probably far—"

She intended to let Carter off the hook because she knew Mags well enough to know her friend wouldn't drop this topic without intervention. Knowing that, along with still getting to know *Carter* meant she needed to step in and do it fast. Carter had been nice to her from the moment he'd met her. He'd saved her from having to devour an entire platter of salad, leaving none for anyone else. He'd come tonight, driving a half hour from his new place the next town over, giving up his Thursday night to listen to her friends blabber about knitting and booze and now Maggie giving him the fifth degree in the vein of trying to get a male opinion about the loser she'd slept with.

But Carter didn't let Misty intervene.

"If a man is any sort of man," Carter said, reaching over and leaning very close to Mags, his face in hers, his expression intense enough to have Misty's heart stuttering, and it wasn't even directed at her, "he doesn't need to ask if he was a good fuck. He *knows* he's a good fuck because the woman he's just fucked is fucking *wrecked* and can't summon the energy to utter a syllable, let alone summon a full comment on his abilities in bed. So no, you weren't wrong to tell him he fucking sucked. You deserve a plethora of fucking orgasms."

Misty's mouth had fallen open.

She wasn't the only one.

Maggie was stunned silent—which was a *fucking feat* considering that Maggie was *never* silent, and certainly not when she'd had a few cosmos.

There was a choked sound that came from the kitchen, and Misty slowly turned and saw that Raven and Frankie were standing there, equally stunned expressions on their faces.

Maggie, no surprise, recovered first.

She stood up, plunked herself into Carter's lap, and said, "Promise me that you'll *fucking wreck* me."

Heat in his hazel eyes, hands clamping on to Maggie's curvy hips.

Misty held her breath, thinking that he was going to haul her close and ravage her friend, thinking that she needed to slide off the couch and away from the armchair they were occupying and hide in her bedroom, snagging Raven and Frankie along the way to give Maggie and Carter privacy for all that *fucking wrecking*.

But Carter didn't pull Maggie closer.

Instead, he set her away from him, his voice gentle but firm when he said, "As gorgeous as you are, honey, I'm seeing someone." Then he stood and started gathering up glasses, disappearing into the kitchen.

The faucet turned on.

It was as though the room was a balloon and someone had just poked it with a pin, all the air hissing out.

Misty looked at Frankie then at Raven then all three of them turned to stare at Maggie.

"Well fuck," Maggie said, her trademark smile in place. "I was hoping to bag myself a Jackson brother. Guess I'll have to live vicariously through you, Misty-moo."

She sank back onto the armchair and started back on the chips.

Easy come. Easy go.

That was Maggie Augustin.

Frankie, thankfully, started the conversation back up, and it got heated quickly because they were deciding which board games of Misty's to play, and the only thing that Frankie took more seriously than knitting was playing board games.

Which meant that by the time Carter emerged from the kitchen, the conversation was far away from sex and firmly entrenched in Sushi Go and who was going to get the most maki rolls.

The loser would be buying pizza.

Thankfully, Carter didn't seem any worse for wear, and he even joined in on a couple of rounds before the girls took off— Raven paged to the hospital, Frankie gathering up her stuff to drive her and Maggie home.

Misty tried to encourage Carter to take off, knowing it was getting late and Chance would be back soon, and she needed to get over this fear of being alone, but he'd ignored her, promising to be back in a couple of minutes because he refused to allow Frankie to drive since she'd partaken in cosmos (though only two of them since she was *healthy*, the nut). Instead, he'd insisted on driving both of them home, asking Misty if she wanted to come with him rather than hanging out at her house by herself.

His concern and, albeit pushy, care had her eyes prickling.

These Jackson men.

It also had Maggie sighing and hugging her tight. "No waterworks tonight, love bug. We've had too much fun, and the only one allowed to cry is Frankie because she lost at Sushi Go."

That was correct, so Misty had blinked her tears away and waited at the house, telling Carter to take her keys with him because she wanted a bath and candle time.

He hadn't missed a beat, just nodded, squeezed her arm, and said, "Be back soon."

Then he'd bustled her friends to the door, which he'd locked, and she'd bustled to the bathroom, relaxing in water that was as hot as she could stand.

A knock had come just as she was stepping in.

"I'm back," Carter said through the door. "Holler if you need anything."

She'd called her thanks, sank into the hot water, so damned glad to not have to worry about getting her cast wet, and then she closed her eyes, rested her head on her bath pillow, and chilled out.

Because she had a Jackson looking out for her.

———

SOMETIME LATER, the door squeaked open.

She jumped, but then Chance poked his head in, eyes hot. "Whatcha doing, Cloudless?"

Her hands had gone to her breasts, between her thighs, preparing to cover up in case of Carter's invasion.

She should have known better.

Carter wasn't the type of guy to barrel into a bathroom unless the house was on fire.

And then he'd probably shout a warning first before launching her robe at her.

Also, yes, she might have been dozing after reading a romance where the main character did exactly that.

Also, yes, it was probably why she asked, "Is the house on fire?"

Mostly wishful thinking—not that she'd lose her house or people would be in danger—but that a sexy fireman might sweep in and rescue her.

Chance's face was adorably confused. "What?"

"Never mind," she murmured, sitting up slightly, dropping her hands into the water.

And she knew that part of his confusion was because she was babbling about fires, but the rest was because he wasn't much focused on the conversation.

His gaze was on her breasts.

She followed it down, saw that with her shifting, they were bobbing in the water, the bubbles mostly gone, her nipples just above the surface. They went all tingly, tightening, and she felt an answering tightening through her womb, moisture gathering between her thighs.

He crossed to her, knelt by the side of the tub. "Hi," he murmured, brushing his lips over hers. "Have to say that I like where your hands were before, baby."

"What?"

He reached into the water, fingers circling her wrist, pressing a kiss to the finally-bared skin, and gently set it on her breast, squeezing it rhythmically until she clued in and took over, massaging herself, thumb brushing over the sensitized tip. Then he grabbed the other hand and placed it back between her thighs.

"Oh," she breathed.

He pressed down slightly, guiding her fingers unerringly to her clit, his fingers joining hers to circle it the way that had her squirming immediately, more moisture flooding her pussy. He stroked through her folds, leaving her to her clit, and then slipped a finger inside her.

"Chance?"

"Mmm?" he asked, that finger sliding in and out of her.

"What are you doing?"

"Finger fucking you while you touch yourself."

Matter of fact words said so baldly it took a moment for her to process them. And when they did, it felt as though her bath water had ratcheted up a thousand degrees, heat flooding through her.

Her hands froze.

That finger inside her curled up, and she gasped as sparks flashed behind her eyes.

"Keep moving, baby, I want to watch you come."

"Carter—"

He bent and nipped her nose. "Not loving you talking about my brother when my fingers are inside you, Cloudless." His mouth tipped up when she gaped at him. "But he's gone. Took off when I got here."

She relaxed. "You said fingers."

"Mmm?"

"You said *my fingers are inside you*," she murmured. "But you only have *one* finger inside me."

A pause. A wicked grin.

Then he slid another inside. "Easily fixed, Cloudless. Now move."

She moved. *He* moved. His mouth found her ear, her jaw, her mouth, her throat. He kept stroking. *She* kept stroking, one hand on her clit, one on her breasts.

And when he bent to suck one nipple into his mouth...she shattered.

Gloriously.

She was still coming when he scooped her out of the bath, still coming when he propped her on the vanity top and thrust inside her, still coming when he found his own orgasm.

By the time she came back to reality, it was to find herself cuddled against his chest, Chance's ass on her plush bathmat, his chest rising and falling rapidly, his arms wrapped around her.

Fuck, that was good.

Not just the sex.

But Chance here on her bathmat. With her in his lap.

It was even better when he scooped her up and carried her to bed.

———

IT'S TOO BAD," she murmured, much later, their naked bodies intertwined as they relaxed in bed, "that the space next to Tangled has been leased. It would be nice to have you next door."

He grinned.

She pushed up on her hands, suspicion trickling through her. "What?"

Tracing circles on her skin, casual as can be, he said, "Well, I may have forgotten to tell you something again."

More suspicion. So, brows dragging together, she asked, "Forgot or didn't?"

Sitting up and bundling her close, he said, "Didn't." A squeeze, probably because he could feel her go stiff as a board. "Mostly because I only got the confirmation yesterday, and then we were fighting about your cast, and then we were *fucking* about your cast, and I was on the road most of the day." He smoothed back her hair and she felt herself soften, mostly because the gentleness in his green eyes made her go all squishy inside. "But I'm telling you now that it's good you think it would be nice to have me next door because I'm *going* to be next door."

It took her a beat to process it.

Then she realized what he'd said. "Really?"

He nodded. "Really."

"That's *so* cool. We can carpool from here together and still have our mornings." He usually made her coffee and got her some variety of baked goods from the bakery so she didn't get tired of cinnamon rolls (not that she seriously thought she *could* get tired of cinnamon rolls, but variety wasn't a bad thing necessarily).

Then she realized what she was saying and assuming.

"I mean," she hurried to add when he opened his mouth, "you could totally be doing your own thing. I know that space has an apartment on top"—and despite his being at her house and having moved out from his apartment in Atlanta, he hadn't really brought more than a duffle bag, some work files, and his laptop to her place over the last six weeks—"so if you're going to stay there, then I'll just see you around and..."

He placed a finger over her bottom lip, silencing her. Then stared at her, those emerald eyes dancing. "I'll just see you around?" he asked.

She winced.

Yeah, that hadn't come out right.

"I—"

"I'm happy to stay in the apartment if you need space," he said, cupping her jaw, "but I'd rather be here with you, Cloudless. I think I've made it clear that I've waited my whole life for a woman like you." He tugged a lock of her hair, lightly, not painfully, and God, she loved when he did that. Because he always smiled at her just like he was smiling at her in that moment—like she'd hung the sun in the sky. "I just didn't want to assume that you'd be open to me moving in, since it hasn't been that long we've been together."

"Thinking of me," she murmured, oddly touched.

"Always," he replied.

"Well, if all the thinking gets me my way, then I vote for you to move in here."

His eyes went warm. "You good with that?"

Still thinking about her.

She snuggled closer to him. "*So* good with that."

"Good," he said, amusement clinging to his voice, "because all my shit is in my car."

Misty froze.

Then started laughing as she pushed off his chest. "Well, let's put this naked arm to good use and go get it."

He caught her around the waist, tumbled her back on the mattress.

"I'd rather put this naked *body* to good use."

His mouth came down to hers, his fingers slipped between her thighs, and...she decided the boxes could wait until morning.

22

APOLOGIES

Chance

"Mмм," Misty said.

Which was pretty much his favorite sound ever, though he had to say, he preferred it when she was naked rather than when she was eating pancakes.

But they were pancakes he'd made her—from scratch—so he was feeling plenty prideful. He was expanding his breakfast cooking abilities.

And making her a second helping, spooning batter onto the griddle, just as the doorbell rang.

He moved to set the bowl and ladle down, but she stood, her plate clean except for leftover syrup—and a large puddle of it, because the only way to eat pancakes was to drown them in syrup. "I've got it," she assured him, crossing to him, kissing him on the cheek, then striding out of the kitchen.

He finished loading the griddle, started watching the bubbles on the backs of the cooking pancakes, and waited to hear voices in the hall—expecting their siblings or her friends or one of the multitude of visitors who'd made it their business to check up on her over the last weeks.

But he didn't hear voices.

He heard *nothing*.

His nape prickled. He dropped the bowl and ladle to the counter, turned off the burners, and took off for the hall.

But his foot had barely made it into the space before he heard Misty scream.

Turning the corner, sprinting toward her, he saw someone in the open door, watched her scramble back and fall on to her ass. He was next to her in a second, lifting her up and shoving her behind him, putting himself between her and...Todd Hanover.

What. The. Fuck?

He pulled his phone out and dialed 9-1-1, lifting it to his ear at the same time as he told Todd, "You need to leave. Now."

Todd put his hands up, palms out, and he stepped back but didn't vacate the porch.

Chance wanted to beat the fucker within an inch of his life for daring to be on Misty's property. But Mist didn't need to see that. She needed to feel safe, and she wouldn't feel safe if he lost his shit and started wailing on Todd. Even if the asshole deserved it. Thankfully, before Chance lost control, the operator picked up and he explained in a rapid clip what was happening, asking them to send a unit as quickly as possible before hanging up.

Because what *wasn't* happening was Todd leaving.

Instead, the sick fuck was staring at Misty, his face pale, his hands still out.

"Get the fuck out of here," Chance growled, stepping to the right, deliberately cutting off the fucker's view of Misty.

"Misty," Todd began. "I just want to—"

Chance lost the hold on his temper. His woman was behind him, and he could practically feel the air rattling around her, she was trembling so hard, her breathing was so loud and rasping. He moved forward, hating that he heard Misty cry out, grabbed Todd fucking Hanover by the collar of his shirt and slammed him against the outside wall of the house. "I don't give a fuck what you want. You don't come here. You don't knock on her door. You don't see *her*."

"I—"

"And I know this is a fucking violation of your bond," he snapped, shaking the asshole like a rag doll, "and because of that, I'd be well within my rights to put another fucking bullet in your gut just for being here on her porch, refusing to leave when asked. But *I* don't hurt women or scare them, and I won't do that to her because she's had enough fucking nightmares about *you*."

Todd went paler, his hands out at his sides. "I just wanted to a-apologize—" He tried to look around Chance, searching for Misty. "I was messed up and out of my mind, Misty. I hurt you. I'm sorry—I just didn't want you to live thinking that I was coming for you and—"

Chance's grip tightened and he shoved Todd harder against the wall. "Except you *did* come, asshole. You're here. Violating another safe space for her. *Hurting* her again."

Todd's eyes closed. "I fucked up," he said. "I *was* fucked up. Desperate for my next fix, not giving a shit about anything but getting high. I—when I woke up in the hospital, handcuffed to the bed and remembered what I'd done, I wanted to die. I *deserved* to die. I'm…well, I'm clean now and going to stay that way, and I'm going to serve my time and when I get out, I will never, *ever* darken your life again, Misty."

Sirens blared.

Tires screeched.

Footsteps echoed across the concrete.

The officers took over, handcuffed Todd, and brought him to the squad car. Chance made sure Todd was secured then moved back to Misty.

She had tears in her eyes, glistening on her cheeks, and her skin was pale, her breathing still heavy.

But she was on her feet, the other officer standing next to

her, and her gaze was on Todd being shoved into the back of the police car.

"Cloudless," he murmured, wrapping his arms around her. He didn't ask if she was okay. He just brought her close, held her tight, and looked at the officer.

"We'll come back tonight for your statements."

Nodding his thanks, he guided Misty into the house, closed and locked the door, then swept her up into his arms and carried her to the couch. She was shaking, but so was he. Because, fuck, it would be so easy to lose her, so easy to not have all this in his life. Easy as opening a door. And maybe he should fucking run, take off and distance himself from this feeling of helplessness and rage and terror, maybe running was the safe call.

But he was in too deep.

He couldn't have left even if someone put a gun to his head.

He didn't *want* to leave.

So, he held her close, smoothed back her hair, ran a hand up and down her spine, and got his own shit under control.

"He won't come near you again," he murmured. "I'll make sure of that."

"I know," she said, and it didn't process at first, but then it did. Her voice was steadier than his. *He* was the one shaking, not her, not any longer. And when she cupped his cheeks and straightened, looking deep in his eyes, the tears were gone, her skin was no longer pale.

"Mist?" he asked.

"I'm okay. I-I—it was wrong for him to come here." More steady. More calm. Her hand stroked his chest, gentling him.

Gentling *him*.

Seriously.

"But I believe him," she continued. "I—he didn't look like the man from that night, his eyes crazed, his face a freaky mask"—a shudder—"he looked like a normal man, and one who wanted to make amends. I can give that to him, give it to myself."

She laughed, and it wasn't quite as bright as normal, but it was laughter.

She was *laughing* after a man who had hurt her showed up on her porch and tried to make amends. And Chance believed him, too. He didn't want to think anything good of that fucker, but if Todd fucking Hanover gave Misty some peace, then he could live with that.

Especially when she laughed quietly again and said, "It's easier to give that to myself when I know he's going to be in jail for a while."

Then she brushed her lips to his, wrapped her arms around his neck, and squeezed. "Thank you for stepping in."

Chance froze, any words he'd hoped to give her stoppering up in his throat.

Because fuck, she was amazing.

Fuck, he was proud of her.

"I love you," he murmured, "and I am so fucking amazed by you."

She straightened, her eyes soft. "I love you, too." A beat. "Now, not to be dismissive of that shit-show on the front porch, but I really could use some more pancakes."

He stilled.

His lips curved.

He busted up.

Then he got on making more pancakes.

———

"THESE ARE AMAZING," his dad said, cramming in another of Misty's cupcakes—his third, for those who were keeping track.

Ben Jackson, former FBI agent, expert at undercover work, and complete and utter chocoholic.

If his dad hadn't loved Misty before for being so awesome to

Soph during her initial move to Stoneybrooke, for being Rob's —who was a good guy down to the marrow of his bones— sister, this would have taken the cake.

No pun intended.

Well, maybe a small one.

And clearly happiness was melting Chance's brain. Because though he'd hardly slept the night Todd fucking Hanover had shown up at Misty's place, wanting to be ready to jump in if she had a nightmare, *she'd* slept like a baby.

Okay, not a baby—or at least not like *him* as a baby, since he'd apparently woken up every hour on the hour for the first year of life—and that had been the first thing his mom had decided to share before the guys and girls had split up, the girls to discuss all things baby (the story his mom shared being the first of that, and the main reason the girls and guys had separated to their respective corners), the guys to drink and consume as much food as possible.

Hence his dad shoving cupcake three in his mouth.

And chasing it with a beer.

"Fuck, that's good," he said on an exhale, rubbing his stomach—which was flat, because even though his dad was older, he still kept himself in good shape. "And totally worth the extra miles on the treadmill."

"That they are," Chance agreed, helping himself to another —only his second, since Mist had made him an entire dozen that she'd stashed in their fridge at home. Thinking of her made his eyes go to her, same as they'd continued to find her during the barbecue, over and over again. She was laughing and beautiful and fuck, he loved her.

He'd moved his boxes into her guest bedroom after the excitement of two days before and before they'd gone down to the police station to give their statements.

Misty had held it together through them, had finally seemed at peace.

And yes, Todd's bond had been revoked, and he'd bought himself a couple of additional years in lockup.

Good for Misty.

Chance didn't give a fuck what it meant for the asshole, other than it meant Misty got a few more years to breathe easy.

"I didn't think you'd get here."

His dad's voice was quiet, almost a whisper.

"What?" he asked, turning to glance up at him.

"Didn't think you'd be able to make yourself vulnerable in the way it takes to love a woman," he elaborated.

And *that* was not where he thought this conversation was going.

Chocolate to vulnerable enough to love.

"I know my injury fucked you up," he said. "And I'm sorry for it."

Those were words Chance had heard before. His family wasn't much for keeping things in, and when it was clear he'd been hit hard after his dad had gotten hurt, was struggling when he went back to work, his parents didn't just pretend it was a phase or something he'd get over. They got him in to talk to someone, and they sat in his room and had numerous conversations to check in with him.

As a preteen, he hadn't loved those conversations.

As an adult male, he found he loved them even less.

But he got the point his dad was making—namely that Chance had expressed interest in Misty from the moment he'd laid eyes on her, that he'd fallen hard and fast, that they'd gotten serious quickly, and now he was living with her in her house and having arguments about splitting the mortgage, insurance, utilities, and property taxes (which they'd been bickering over—Misty saying she didn't need help with it, so he should focus on setting up his office, and him saying he could easily do both and if he was staying with her, it wouldn't be on a free fucking ride—when they'd walked into his parents' house earlier that afternoon).

"I can't say it didn't shake me," he told his dad. "You were a superhero to me, and superheroes aren't supposed to get hurt. I saw Mom...saw how it affected her, how scared she was, even though she was trying to hold it together, and I never wanted to put a family through it."

Quiet, then, "I get that."

"But what I didn't realize was that it could go the other way, too."

"That night in Misty's shop," his dad murmured.

Chance nodded. "That's when I realized *I* could be the one left behind. *I* could lose it all. I liked her before. Hell, I probably loved her already, but when I saw her bloody and broken with that fucker holding a baseball bat over her head, I knew that even if something happened to one of us, I would never regret a moment of our time together."

"You never had that before."

"No," he said, shaking his head. "Before Misty, I had never met someone who made me know it could be worth the risk. But from the moment I met her, I knew that she was different, that *I* could be different with her."

His dad clapped him on the shoulder, grinned. "Well, I'm glad you finally got your head out of your ass."

Chance snorted. "Thanks, Dad."

A squeeze, his voice taking on a hint of gentleness. "Because you deserve it. You deserve the good and the woman who looks at you with open adoration and the full life, Chance, and I'm so glad you finally saw that."

Fuck, now Chance was ready to cry.

He stared at the women, at the laughter and love on display. Soph so happy even though she'd been traumatized and closed-off just a year before. His mom ruling court. His woman fitting right in and unscathed and joyful.

Fucking beautiful.

All of it.

But most especially...Misty.

And somehow sensing that his emotions were raw, Misty glanced up and met his eyes. She was on her feet in an instant, coming over to him and slipping her arm around his waist, rising on tiptoe to kiss his cheek, and murmuring in his ear, "You okay?"

"That right there, son," his dad said softly, clapping him on the shoulder again. "*That* right there."

Chance knew exactly what his dad meant.

Which was why he tugged Misty close, murmured in *her* ear, "I love you," and then stuck close to her the rest of the night.

Even though that meant he had to listen to the birth stories.

Misty was tucked into his side.

So all that gore was totally worth it.

23

TISSUES

Misty

"WHAT DO YOU THINK?" she asked, holding up the swatches of color.

Not any shade of purple, as Chance had commanded.

But a nice blue-gray and a rich tan color. Both of which screamed P.I. to her, but what did she know about decorating a private detective's office?

She knew about yarn, and she let that and the wicker do the talking for her in Tangled, aside from her fabulous purple accents, but she didn't know much about interior design.

"I don't care," Chance said, not bothering to look at the samples.

Misty was prepared for this eventuality, because she'd experienced plenty of Chance's "I don't cares" over the last couple of weeks. Aside from setting up his computer and getting the internet and electricity rolling, he couldn't *care* less that the space needed fresh paint and the floor needed mopping. He didn't have a receptionist—yet, he'd said, though he didn't seem to be in any hurry to hire one—mostly because he was working on a new case and had been pulling long enough hours that she'd brought him dinner twice this week then had gone home.

Not that she minded.

Heaven knew she worked late and often too much—so much so that Chance had ordered *her* to hire some help, and she'd countered by telling him she'd get a shop assistant when he hired a receptionist.

Hello, Control Freak One, meet Control Freak Two.

So now they both had interviews the following week—her for a couple of high school girls to close on the evenings she didn't teach classes and to man the shop on the weekends (maybe she'd even open on Sundays permanently, if they worked out), him with two women and a man who had scheduling and billing and other receptionist experience.

The end goal being they would have more time together.

Because they'd been spoiled during her recovery.

All that one-on-one time, him always in her shop, always home, and she'd gotten used to having him right there. Of course, he was still *right there*, considering he spent most of his days next door to Tangled.

It was just that his case was heating up, and he'd spent a couple of nights apart from her while investigating a prescription drug ring.

Apparently, doctors were illegally prescribing, and they had some pharmacists in on it, and then the meds were ending up being sold on the street.

Chance was doing his best to stop it.

Which meant he'd spent some time away from her.

She was getting over her fear of being alone.

Which, yes, it sucked, but it also meant he was doing something pretty damned incredible and making the world a better place. So, the nights and days he was gone, she focused on her work and the booties and sweaters and hats she was knitting for Soph and Rob's baby (the kid was going to be *stocked up*), and spending time with Raven, Frankie, and Maggie.

Maggie, who'd been unusually quiet for the last few weeks. Raven and Frankie, who were their normal selves, and Misty knew that something was going on with her friend but hadn't been able to get it out of her yet.

But soon, maybe.

That night, maybe.

Because Chance was going to meet a contact, so she was hosting ladies' night, and they were going to eat pizza and baked goods she didn't bake and get drunk on cosmos, and then she was going to collapse into bed, wait for Chance to get home, which would hopefully be when she was still tipsy, so she could have wild, tipsy sex with him.

Then they'd sleep the day away because it was Sunday and until she had her teenage helpers, Tangled was closed on Sundays.

She had it all planned out.

But she needed the man to pick a paint color, so she could kiss him goodbye, go to the hardware store before it closed, come back to Tangled to teach her evening class, and then have her ladies' night.

Then have tipsy sex.

A full afternoon and evening, see?

So, the man needed to pick a paint color.

Because Rob was coming tomorrow to sand down and refinish the floor, and the painters were coming in after him. By tomorrow evening, the space wouldn't be decorated, but it would have good bones, and it would look professional for any clients that Chance was going to meet there.

Which was why she tapped her foot and sighed (note: Chance did not look up at this sigh), then pulled out the big guns. "All right," she said, "the lavender it is."

"That's good," he said. "Wait—lavender? Mist." He finally looked at her, jumping up from his desk.

She picked up her purse, started for the door. "It'll look

gorgeous. I'll get some plum throw rugs and maybe a violet vase and—*oh!*"

Chance scooped her up, tossed her over his shoulder, and plunked her onto his desk. "No lavender," he muttered, and snatched the paint swatches from her, looked at them for approximately one-half of a millisecond. "This one," he said, stabbing a finger onto the blue-gray one (for the record, that would have been her choice, too). Then he tossed them on the desk, wove his fingers into her hair, tilted her head back, and glared into her eyes. "You are in *so* much trouble," he muttered.

"Why?" she breathed.

"Because you're too fucking sexy when you're mischievous, and now I have to kiss you. Which means I'm going to want to fuck you. Which means I'm going to be late leaving for my contact, and I can't be late leaving for my contact."

Her pulse had risen, speeding along her veins like cars on a highway. "Then don't kiss me." And yes, she was breathless because she really *really* wanted him to kiss her.

"Fucking can't *not* kiss you, Cloudless."

And then he did kiss her.

And then he was right about needing to fuck her, just as *she* needed *him* to fuck *her*.

And so, he fucked her in his office chair, her sitting astride him, her on top since that was easier for her to come (*ha*), her grinding and rocking against him, crying out when her orgasm hit her, because it was *damned* easy for her to come, both because she was on top, but also because Chance was a really good kisser and always seemed to be able to get her halfway to completion just by having his lips on hers.

And he was right about leaving late.

Because *she* left late for the hardware store, barely able to summon the strength in her legs after they'd cleaned up, dressed, and said a proper goodbye (read: made out like teenagers by Chance's car) to carry the paint cans to her car.

But she summoned that Herculean strength and did it with a smile on her face.

Because Chance Jackson was in her life, and it was pretty fucking great.

"OKAY, SPILL."

Misty blinked.

Because that had been directed at Maggie, but it hadn't originated from Misty—though Maggie's moping had Misty making plans to pull her into the kitchen for a quiet chat.

That was, before Frankie had spoken up.

Not Raven. Not Misty.

But Frankie, who was about as far from confrontational as one could be.

Mags got this, too. She paled and picked up her glass but didn't drink from it.

Come to think of it, she hadn't been drinking from it. Hadn't gotten a refill. It was as full as it had been from when Raven had filled it with their first round of cosmos.

The glass plunked down onto the table.

Mags' breathing sped up, so fast Misty barely understood her when she said, "I'm pregnant."

Silence.

Processing.

Then the four of them spoke at once.

"Breathe, Mags." Raven.

"Oh my God." Frankie.

"Are you okay?" Misty.

And perhaps, most importantly, from Maggie herself. "It's the bad lay's."

"The one you told was bad?" Misty asked, reaching over and squeezing her friend's hand.

Mags groaned then nodded. "He's the only one I've slept

with in the last few months." She swallowed. "And he signed papers to relinquish his parental rights this morning."

Fuck.

"Mags." She squeezed her hand again. "Are you okay?"

Maggie finally looked at Misty, and she shook her head. "I don't think I am. I'm—I'm keeping the baby, but maybe I shouldn't. I don't know how to be a parent. I didn't even have parents."

Misty smothered a wince.

Maggie had, of course, had parents, but they'd taken off before her first birthday, and then her grandparents had raised her. But they were gone now, and neither of them had been particularly flowery and lovey while Mags had been growing up, and Maggie had spent the majority of her time at Frankie's and Misty's houses.

So, in a way, she *hadn't* had parents.

"You're a great friend," Misty said, gripping Mags' hand when it looked like she was going to run. "You love without reservation, you're generous and funny and kind, and I know those are the key characteristics in being a parent, so you've got a leg up."

Mags sniffed. Then, "I don't want to be like them."

"You won't," she promised.

"How do you know?"

Frankie came close now. "Because you care enough to *not* want to be like them."

Raven squeezed in. "I agree," she said. "I know I'm relatively new to town, but I've seen and treated a lot of people. You caring about a baby who's not even here yet means that you're better off than most."

Mags' mouth parted on an exhale, her bottom lip trembling. "You really think so?"

"I know so." Raven nodded firmly. "Now, have you seen your obstetrician?"

Mags shook her head. "No. My normal doctor did a blood

test to confirm the one I took at home, but I have an appointment tomorrow. I—maybe I should have seen her first, but she was booked, and when I told Steve about the positive test, he freaked out, told me to get rid of it." Her lip trembled again. "So, I knew that I didn't want him in the baby's life. Especially when he signed the papers the moment I presented them to him and all but told me to get out of his sight. I mean, I get I was a bitch about the orgasm thing, but...this is about an innocent baby."

That right there was why Mags would be a good mom.

"Oh, Mags," Frankie murmured, hugging her tight.

"So, that's why I've been so off," she said. "Aside from feeling like I need to puke my guts up every fucking second, I... pregnant. I mean, fuck. I've taken birth control for fifteen years. I always make the guys wear condoms anyway because...accidents happen. And somehow I'm pregnant and I-I—"

The waterworks came then and considering Misty was a pro hand at waterworks, she was easily able to leap to action.

Tissues within arm's reach.

A soothing hand rubbing up and down Mags' back.

Frankie was just as good.

She held tight, stroked Mags' hair.

And Raven dove in, sweeping the glasses away and heading into the kitchen. Misty glanced up and saw she was filling her kettle with water, putting it on the stove, and opening cabinets until she located the mugs.

She approved.

Especially since it meant that she could stay next to Mags and be on tissue duty.

By the time the tea was ready and Raven was back with four mugs, Maggie had gotten herself under control. Her face was splotchy, half a box of tissues had been consumed, but she was coming back into herself.

"The nursery is going to be filled with sparkles," she said, sipping at the tea. "I don't care if it's a boy or girl."

"It doesn't matter if the baby is a boy or a girl," Misty told. "Sparkles are good in either scenario."

Frankie nodded. "Misty's right."

Mags smiled. "Of course, she is."

"What will you put with the sparkles?" Misty asked. "Will you find out the gender and go full blue or pink? Or will you do something else like lavender or green or yellow?"

Maggie's eyes started sparkling. "I think lavender and yellow."

"I can fully get behind lavender," Misty said.

Her friend laughed, finally sounding normal again. "Of course, you can, you purple addict."

And Mags was back, and then she was excited. Then they were talking all things baby, and Misty was promising to invite Maggie over next time she saw Soph, so she could get *all* the advice.

Before long, Maggie was yawning—no surprise considering the stress she'd carried the last few weeks and the emotional night. Frankie gathered her up, having driven her over, and took her home, Raven following and promising to meet Maggie for her appointment if she wanted.

"Really?" Maggie asked.

"Of course," Raven said. "I'm there anyway. I'll take my lunch during that time, and so long as there isn't an emergency to cover, I'll come up and meet you."

Maggie started crying again.

More tissues were used.

Hugs were exchanged.

Then the girls were gone, and Misty's house was quiet.

And Misty wasn't tipsy, wasn't going to have tipsy sex with Chance later. But she'd gotten to the bottom of what was going on with Maggie, and it was a doozy, but it would all be okay.

So, *she* was okay.

She was even more okay when Chance called while she was in the bathtub.

"Hi, baby," she murmured. "On your way home?"

His voice was tense. "This is going to take longer than I'd expected," he said. "I'm sorry."

"Everything okay?"

He sighed. "It's all fine. My contact is feeling gun-shy, so I need to wait him out."

"That sucks."

"Sure does," he muttered. "I was supposed to be driving home to meet my sexy and maybe somewhat drunk girlfriend, and when she's maybe somewhat drunk, she likes to blow me—"

"I like to blow you anytime."

He chuckled. "That's what a man loves to hear."

She was grinning. "I know." Then when he didn't say anything else, asked, "Do you need to go?"

"Not for a few minutes. What's up?"

She told him about Maggie and the pregnancy, about Mags' fears and her upbringing, about the tissues and freak out and the bad lay already signing away his rights.

"Whoa. Maggie doesn't play."

"I know." She didn't. "Helps that she's a lawyer and can draft her own paperwork."

"I thought that she worked at one of the stores in town."

"She does. The bakery. She hated being a lawyer, so Mags started working there, but even though she doesn't regularly use her law degree, she still knows how to get her legal ducks in a row."

"That's a nice side-benefit."

It was.

They talked for a few more minutes, not about Maggie and the pregnancy or her former lawyering, but about the plans for the next couple of days. Tomorrow they were going to go down to the beach and just hang, just the two of them, then maybe meet up with Rob and Soph for a late lunch. Monday, she'd teach, and he was going to work late so they could go home together. Tuesday, they were going to see a movie and go out to dinner.

"And you're not stealing any popcorn of mine unless you let me buy a giant ass tub," he grumbled.

She rolled her eyes. *One time* she'd accidentally finished his popcorn. She'd just wanted a taste. Jeez. "Do you know how many calories movie theater popcorn has?"

"Do you *know* how little I care? We're at the movies. It's time to indulge and not worry about calories."

Since that was a good point, she stopped arguing. "Fine," she muttered. "You can get the large popcorn."

"Extra-large," he muttered.

Laughter in her veins. "Extra-large," she confirmed. "But no grumbling when I eat half of it," she muttered to counter *his* mutter.

"Fine." She could tell he was smiling, but then his voice went serious. "Cloudless, babe, I've got to go."

"Okay."

"I'll be there beside you when you wake up in the morning."

"All right, baby. Love you."

"I love you, too."

Then he hung up.

Then she finished her bath.

Then she went to bed with a huge smile on her face.

SUNLIGHT POURING through the windows woke her up.

She was still smiling, still so freaking in love with Chance that she found herself with a lovestruck grin on her face from dusk to dawn.

Half-asleep, she rolled, intending to burrow into his side, knowing that if they drifted apart while sleeping, they always cuddled back up when one of them awoke.

But her roll only brought her to cold sheets, a cool pillow.

"What?" she murmured, instantly awake.

She pushed up, studied the empty half of the bed, knowing instantly that Chance hadn't been back the night before.

Her stomach knotted, and she grabbed her cell, hoping for a text or a call telling her that he was running late.

But there was nothing from him.

More knotting.

She pushed up, searched the bedroom for a note, then the bathroom, the kitchen, the living room, the bulletin board by the garage, the granola bar basket.

No notes.

"Fuck," she whispered, and there wasn't even a niggle that he'd left her or hadn't come home because he didn't want to or was cutting and running. They were so far beyond that; it didn't even register.

Maybe it should have. They were new and had dived into the deep end.

But it didn't.

Because she and Chance were different, important, more. *True.*

Because the only thing she felt was dread.

Something was wrong.

And it became even more wrong when she tried to call his cell and it went immediately to voicemail.

No. No. This wasn't right.

She called the only person she could think of.

Detective Hopkins.

Then told him about the case—or at least the little she knew, which as he started asking questions, she realized was absolutely nothing. She didn't know where he was meeting his contact, only that it was about two hours away. Didn't know the contact's name. Didn't know what police department he was working with.

She knew *nothing.*

But Detective Hopkins took her seriously.

He told her to stay by her phone, said he would make some calls, and that he would trace Chance's cell.

"I'll call you as soon as I hear something," he promised. "It's probably nothing, honey. But it doesn't hurt to make sure, especially since he's a reliable guy."

He was.

That was why her insides were twisted into a fucking knot.

"Hang in there," Detective Hopkins said. Then he hung up.

And Misty was left hanging.

All morning.

All afternoon.

All fucking evening.

24

BOOTS

Chance

HE STIFLED a groan and slitted his eyes open.

Dark.

Super helpful that.

But with his head pounding and the dim light, he was struggling. One slow breath in. One slow breath out.

Open again.

Okay, not pitch black.

There were windows on the far side of the space—large enough to tell him that instead of being outside the cluster of warehouses where he'd been waiting for his contact, he was now *inside* one of them. It was dark outside, and the throbbing on his head told him he'd been out for a while.

He took a careful inventory of his body.

Ankles were tied to chair legs. Wrists secured behind the back of it. Rope twined around his abdomen and chest.

Not gagged.

Not blindfolded.

Shifting slowly—not that he had much space to do a whole lot of that—he tested the bindings. They were tight enough that he'd lost feeling in his hands and feet, but the slight wiggle room near his hips told him that his wallet, cell, and keys were gone.

Along with his gun.

So, not great.

But focusing on how *not great* things were looking wasn't going to do shit, so he focused on something else—that being, moving his fingers. And then his toes.

It didn't feel great, that prickling, tingling sensation, but he kept with those slow movements until all feeling had returned. Which was good and bad. Because with sensation returning, pain was also coming back, and if someone hadn't been restrained before—and for what was seeming to be for quite a while, considering the amount of pain currently in his limbs—he could clue them into it not feeling great.

Sometimes numb was better.

But numb wasn't going to get him out of this.

Chance took his mind off the pain by focusing on the space around him, his night vision coming in clearer, the shadows revealing themselves slowly. A rack of shelves on the far wall, just beneath the windows. Not empty, perhaps a weapon to be found, if he could make it there. But that wouldn't be easy, or quiet, if he had to shuffle his way over. So not ideal.

He kept looking.

Door on the opposite side of him. Closer than the windows. But still seeming pretty far, considering he was tied to a chair.

Behind him, another rack, close enough that it might be useful, especially if he could get the bindings around the damaged corner with a sharp metal piece sticking out and start hacking at the plastic.

In front of him, a long hallway with voices coming down it.

Closing his eyes, he went limp, and listened really fucking close.

The footsteps came closer.

"...and you need to move the product quickly. If he got this close, that means he knows too much."

Chance had gotten close, that was true. When he'd finally managed to connect with his contact, he'd found out that the lead he'd been teasing out wasn't just a tease. It was *the* lead. And that lead was that the manager at the facility where the local PD kept their evidence was dirty, and he'd gotten it in him to make a quick buck by skimming evidence off the top and fudging their labels and entries in the system.

Made easier because this PD hadn't transitioned fully to electronic records.

Not to mention, he'd helped himself to those drugs slated for incineration, marking them as destroyed but carting them off in his truck after hours instead.

Chance had sent that information off to the department, along with the samples of the fudged records his contact had rummaged up. They could close the case on that alone. But then, since he was close and was already late meeting Misty, knowing she would be asleep by the time he drove the two hours home, he had decided to follow up on his final lead, wanting to get some pictures, to catch the manager red-handed, and make it as easy as possible for the case to be prosecuted.

So, he'd gone to do some recon.

At the warehouses.

Which the manager of the evidence facility was dumb enough to lease under his own name.

Which meant that Chance had gotten cocky.

Because what kind of dumb fuck stole evidence, housed it in a warehouse leased under his own name? Leased! Not even owned, because seriously, what would happen if the landlord came in and found pallets of drugs—because also seriously, the amount of evidence they'd finally tracked down as missing was in the hundreds to thousands of pounds, not something that was easy to hide or conceal.

He'd been snapping pictures when he'd sensed the movement behind him.

A scuff of a boot.

He'd spun.

And then everything had gone black.

Now, he was awake with a splitting headache and tied to a chair.

Sure glad he went for that recon now.

"I saw what was on his camera, Bobby," the voice snapped. "I know it needs to be dealt with. We're ready to move. We just need to deal with this fucker first."

Even more glad for that recon.

Fuck.

The footsteps slowed. The two men were right in front of him, but Chance stayed limp and just barely slit open his eyes. Two pairs of feet in front of him—one a pair of boots, like those a police officer might wear. The other, wingtips—fucking expensive *wingtips*—and he knew those belonged to Bobby, the warehouse manager.

Because the man wasn't exactly subtle with the suits he wore, with the shoes he wore, with the wealth he sported (in gold watches, sports cars, and a big ass house)—much more than he would make as a facilities manager.

The officer—or at least that was who Chance was assuming the other boots belonged to—stepped close and he braced, knowing what was coming.

Pain in his shin, radiating up his legs, rattling his teeth.

The fucker had kicked him.

He forced himself to stay limp, even though those boots appeared to have steel toes. Fucking hell, that hurt. As did the backhand to the face, splitting his lip, jerking his head to the side.

"Fuck, McCannon, how hard did you hit him before?" Manager Bobby said.

"Hard enough."

McCannon. McCannon. Chance tried to go through the names on the roster of the department while hanging there limp, the two men discussing the details on the move. He focused on absorbing those, too, along with breathing slow and deep, staying relaxed, going through the names from the list of officers he'd pulled early on in the investigation.

Because when evidence went missing, typically there was a person on the inside.

He'd found them.

Two people.

Rolf. That was the dumbass's first name. Rolf McCannon.

And Bobby Hoyden.

And he knew where they were taking the drugs. Farmhouse off Old Crenshaw Road outside of town.

Now, to stay alive long enough to get that information to the police.

25

SHOULD HAVES

Misty

It was after ten at night.

She was beside herself.

She'd heard nothing aside from a text a few hours ago from Detective Hopkins, telling her they were still looking into it.

Which meant they had nothing.

Nothing.

And she was done hearing nothing, done *doing* nothing, done *having* nothing.

Which was why she had used the key Chance had given her to go into his office, why she'd just spent the last twenty minutes trying to get into his computer.

And finally succeeding.

His password was Cloudless.

Yes, that would have filled her with joy if not for the fact that her man was missing and no one could find him.

She began looking through his files, knowing it was an invasion of privacy but willing to do whatever was necessary to find him, even if that meant he wouldn't forgive her for it later. Most of the files were password protected, so she didn't have much luck, especially since they were named with some system she couldn't decipher.

Heart sinking, she turned to the internet browser, not having much hope that he hadn't already cleared his search history. He had. But she also saw that he still had a tab open. It was just showing a random browser, but she tried hitting the back arrow, just in case. That was pretty much the extent of her computer sleuthing abilities.

But to her surprise, it worked.

Loading a map, directions from his office to an address.

Searching the desktop, she found a pad and wrote it down. Then hit the back arrow again. It brought her right back to the same search engine she'd started with.

Shit.

But it was something.

She picked up her phone, called Detective Hopkins, and was met with his voicemail. After leaving a message with the address and an explanation of how she'd found it, she spent a few more minutes searching his desk and not finding anything.

"Fuck," she hissed, sitting in his chair, her hands in her hair. "Fucking *hell.*"

What did one do when her boyfriend went missing and his work was potentially dangerous? She'd called the police. She'd gotten them looking. So, what now?

Fuck.

Fuck.

If only she was a fucking secret agent or knew one or—

Carter. Ben.

They were both, or at least in Ben's case, *had been* FBI agents.

They had resources. They had training. They—

Fuck, she should have called them sooner. Oh God, *why* hadn't she called them sooner?

Snatching her phone out of her pocket, she grabbed her purse and ran for the door. Ben and Martha lived close by. Carter farther. She'd call Carter on the way to Ben's.

So, she did that.

The phone rang a couple of times before a female voice picked up. "Hello?"

"Hi, um, is this Carter's phone?" Misty asked, jumping into her car.

"Yes." But there was question in the woman's voice, a question that said she didn't much like the fact that Carter was receiving a call from a random woman after ten at night.

"This is Misty, his brother's girlfriend. Can I talk—?"

"Anika," he heard Carter say, voice slightly muffled. "What are you doing?"

"She says she's your brother's girlfriend." Her tone made it clear she hadn't believed Misty.

"Misty?"

A sigh.

And no offense, Anika sounded like a bitch.

Then there was a scuffle, and Carter's voice came in loud and clear. "Misty. Are you okay?"

"No," she said and tried to explain the situation as quickly as possible. Carter was absolutely silent. "And I'm so fucking stupid. I called Detective Hopkins, but I never even thought about calling you or Ben. I should have—I just thought, I don't know, that I was overreacting, or it wasn't as big of a deal as I worried it was, but if something happened because I-I—" She broke off, near tears and knowing this was not the time for stupid tears.

"Mist?"

"Yeah?"

"Breathe, babe."

"Babe?" she heard screeched in the background.

And yeah, Anika was a bitch.

"Okay," Misty said, blinking back the tears and sucking in some air. "I'm breathing," she whispered.

"I want you to go to my mom and dad's place. Tell my dad everything you told me, okay?"

"Okay," she said again. "I'm already driving there."

"Good girl." And somehow the use of *good girl* didn't piss her off. It just calmed her enough to take another breath. "Now, give me the address again."

She gave him the address.

"I'll find him, sweetheart. I promise."

Then he hung up.

Then she drove to Ben and Martha's.

———

BEN HAD LISTENED to her as silently as Carter had before turning for the hall and grabbing a gun, a jacket, and a pair of boots.

He'd kissed Martha.

Then had asked for the address.

And then had disappeared out the door.

"I'm so sorry," she told Martha. "I should have come to you guys this morning. I-I'm so fucking stupid and—"

"Stop." Martha squeezed her hand. "You didn't sit on your butt and do nothing. You called the police, first thing. They should have reached out to us if they thought our son was missing. I don't know why they didn't, because that's standard operating procedure, but you"—another squeeze—"are not a police officer. You can't expect to have acted like one."

"He's your son," she countered. "I should have called you."

"Misty, baby. If, God forbid, Chance ever goes missing again, you'll know just what to do. But going over and over this in your mind isn't going to help anyone."

Misty blew out a breath. "You're right."

"Of course, I am," Martha said with a small smile that didn't hide the worry in her eyes, and Misty felt a burn of guilt for making Martha comfort *her* when Chance was missing. It should be the other way around, since Chance was her son. Or they should be comforting each other. Or—

"Chance is really good at what he does," Misty blurted. "I'm sure he's fine."

"Of course, he is."

But Misty didn't miss that neither of them sounded convinced.

———

NO WORD.

Still no word from anyone.

Martha had gone to bed a little bit before, but Misty didn't think Chance's mom was actually going to sleep. Instead, it seemed like she needed a moment.

Which was fine.

Misty needed one, too.

She was sitting on Martha and Ben's front porch, smelling the salt of the ocean, feeling the cool air on her skin, and searching the street, hoping that Chance might just pull into the driveway and be miraculously fine.

But as the hours went on and the sky began to lighten, Chance still didn't show.

26

OVERLORD

Chance

A NOISE AT HIS RIGHT.

Bobby and Rolf had come back twice, and Chance knew he couldn't keep pretending to be asleep.

They were either just going to kill him, or they'd realize he was faking...and kill him.

Good times.

But he'd managed to shift the chair toward the rack, and now he was sawing his way through his restraints.

Or had been.

Because the noise had him freezing.

He played at unconscious, since that was pretty much his only option at this point.

"Chance."

His brother's voice.

He blinked, slitted his eyes, and saw Carter emerge out of the shadows. He wanted to ask how in the fuck he was there, but this wasn't the time for questions. It was time for a quick imparting of information and then quiet.

"Two guys back office. One for sure armed. I'm restrained

ankles and wrists and torso."

Carter was already moving.

And then he saw another shadow emerge, just behind Carter.

"Dad?" he breathed.

A nod and then he came over and knelt to cut Chance's restraints. "Misty."

For a second, he thought that meant Misty was in danger, and his heart seized. Then he looked into his dad's eyes and realized it was the answer to the question he hadn't voiced earlier. Misty was how they were there.

"Let's move," Carter said as their dad sliced through the rope at Chance's waist.

Chance didn't need to be told twice. He stood, shoved off the rope, and stood. Pins and needles, stiff as fuck, but he got his shit together and followed Carter when he started to lead them out of the building, his dad bringing up the rear.

Quiet.

Too quiet as they ran across the parking lot, following Carter and putting distance between them and the warehouse.

And he knew why he felt that way when the moment they hit the parking lot, footsteps exploded in front of them, spotlights flaring to life and blinding him, and then people—no, officers and agents—swarmed into the building. He froze for a second, but his dad shoved him forward. "Move."

Gunshots rang out.

Voices kept yelling.

His dad pushed him until he cleared the other side of a vehicle—*his* vehicle, he realized as they rounded the SUV.

"Fuck, kid," he muttered, throwing an arm around Chance and yanking him close. "You scared the shit out of me."

"*I* scared the shit out of me," he said, enduring the hug and smothering his wince. "How?"

"Misty was worried, called the detective from her case. He started tracking you down, since she didn't have specifics. He got the ping on your cell back about the time that Misty broke into your computer, found this address, and called Carter and me."

Chance's brows rose.

Carter shrugged. "I was here first, talked to the units—" The noise behind them faded. "They were tracking the movements inside, watching them load up the trucks, and wanted to make sure all parties were caught, but didn't know where you were. We all did recon, we spotted you, and Dad showed up. Got you. They were ready to go in." Another shrug, this time paired with a jerk of his chin behind them. "They went in."

Chance glanced behind them, saw Bobby in his wingtips being wrestled out, Rolf handcuffed behind him.

"Thanks to your little sleeping act," Carter said, "and nice one, by the way, I watched you fool them through the windows up top. The bad guys stayed around, and we were able to catch them moving the product."

At that point, the detective Chance had worked with came up, bulletproof vest strapped on, and was shoving his gun into his holster. "I think you went above and beyond closing this case for us," Ron said, shaking his hand. His gaze apparently took in Chance's wrists, which were sore as fuck and crusty with blood. "Need a medic?"

Chance shook his head. "I'm good. Want to take my statement so I can get the fuck out of here?"

He needed to get home, needed to call Misty.

Needed some real fucking sleep.

"On it."

Chance gave his statement, learned that his SUV, phone, and wallet would be evidence for a few more days. Great.

Then he got in his brother's car.

Carter's because he didn't want to deal with the lecture that his dad was going to give him, namely that he should always have a backup for this kind of work, or at least let someone know where he was going.

All of which were right.

None of which he wanted to hear in that moment.

"Should I just tell Dad I gave you the lecture?" Carter asked.

"That would be preferred," Chance muttered.

"Backup, yeah?"

Fuck.

"Yeah."

The silence stretched then, "Want a partner?"

Chance sighed. "I get the checking in and needing backup, Carter. I won't fuck up like this again."

His brother turned on to the freeway heading toward Stoneybrook. "That's not what I meant." His fingers clenched on the steering wheel. "I'm getting out. I'm done with the bureaucracy and bullshit. I'm tired of taking cases I have to, and I want to work on those I'm interested in. So"—he glanced at Chance—"I'm seriously asking if you want a partner."

Work with his brother?

He considered that. "You going to move to Stoneybrook or close?"

"Yeah."

"Anika, too?" A long-distance (even if that distance was just about an hour) would be a tough sell for what he knew of his brother's woman. Beautiful, but needy, and with a hint of self-ish. She hadn't once made the drive to Stoneybrook to meet the family, even though they'd been dating six months and Carter came almost once a week.

A beat then, "Anika and I are done."

That wasn't exactly a surprise, but Chance couldn't say he was broken up about it. He wanted Carter to find the same thing he had.

"So, partner?" Chance asked when Carter's tone made it clear he didn't want to discuss Anika any further.

Carter shrugged. "Why not?"

That was a good question. Carter certainly had the skills, was smart, that wasn't in doubt. But, "You sure you want to work for me? You know I'm small-time, right? It's not like I'm doing the big takedowns like the FBI."

"Tonight wasn't a big takedown?"

Well, he had a point.

"Okay, but I'm just saying, the department took care of it. Yeah, I do the drug cases, but I also occasionally do cheating and tracking down family members. It's definitely not all gunfights and kidnappings."

Carter glanced at him. "I'm not all that down with gunfights or kidnappings, especially if they involve my brother."

Well, damn, he had another point.

"Who's in charge?" Chance asked.

"You are." No hesitation. "You built it. You're just letting me ride on your coattails."

Chance laughed. "Works for me. But I'm good with partners."

"I bet you'd be better with Underling, Overlord."

More laughter.

Then Chance's laughter cut off as he remembered where he was, what had happened, and what Misty had done. Fuck, he was sitting there chitchatting, and his woman was worried at home. "Can I use your phone?"

A nod to the cupholder where his phone sat.

He unlocked the screen, dialed Misty, and—

"Carter?" Her voice was frantic.

"Hi, Cloudless."

"Are you okay?"

"Fine, baby."

"I love you," she breathed.

"I love you, too."

His brother stilled but didn't comment, just drove in silence, his eyes on the road, though Chance sensed his smile.

Her breath slid out on a long exhale. Then that voice went sharp. "What the fuck were you thinking not telling anyone where you were going? I've been freaking out all day and—"

"Baby."

"—and your mom is worried and—"

"*Baby.*"

"I woke up and you weren't there—"

Her voice broke.

Shit.

"Misty, baby. I'm sorry. I promise it won't happen again. I'll take backup and make sure someone always knows where I am, and you won't wake up without knowing where I am again. I swear to you."

Her breaths still came rapidly, but she'd stopped yelling.

"Okay?" he said. "I promise. And Carter is going to work with me so that we can watch each other's backs, and all will be good."

Silence.

Then, "Okay."

"I'll be home soon."

"I'm at your parents' house."

"All right, I'll be there soon. Okay?"

A deep breath. "Okay."

"Love you."

"Love you, too."

He hung up, put the phone back in the cupholder.

Carter was quiet for a long time.

Then he said, "Why do I feel like that was worse for you than being on the receiving end of Dad's lecture?"

Chance laughed. "Because it was."

"Good thing your Underling's got your back."

"I think I'm going to get a plaque with Overlord on it."

Carter chuckled. "I'll order you one myself."

"Consider the Underling one I'll be getting you your signing bonus."

They busted up.

And the shittiest night of his life ended up not being so bad.

27

TISSUES TIMES TWO

Misty

"YOU WERE out of contact for nearly twenty-four hours!" she snapped when Chance tried again to make light of what had happened.

He had bruises on his wrists, and the bruises had cuts, and his ankles were just as bad.

And that didn't include his black eye, his split lip, and the cautious way he moved that spoke of bruised ribs.

"What?" he asked, brows drawing together. "Twenty-four—?"

"Yes, my love," she said—or rather still snapped, "this is not you being a few hours late. This is you being twenty-*four* hours late."

They were back at her house, cuddled up in her bed after she'd slapped about a dozen bandages on various parts of his body, and she was just holding on to him and trying not to freak out.

"I'm fine, Cloudless."

"You fussed over me, Chance, so I'm fussing over you."

He smoothed back her hair. "You were a bad patient. You hardly tolerated the fussing at all."

"Newsflash, so are you. As in, you're not tolerating it *at all*."

"Because there's nothing to fuss about."

"You were *kidnapped*," she pointed out.

"I didn't get hit with a baseball bat," he countered.

"No," she muttered, "just with someone's fist. Repeatedly."

He cupped her cheek. "Should we talk about something else?"

"Are you going to tolerate my fussing?"

"No."

An inhale. An exhale. "*Chance.*"

"Okay, you allowed me two days of fussing after getting knocked out and earning a broken wrist"—she snorted at the thought of "earning a broken wrist"—"so my getting knocked out and sitting on my ass for twenty-four hours means I'll allow you..."

"Four—" she began.

"Hours," he finished.

Her mouth fell open.

"*What?*"

He glanced at the clock on the nightstand. "And look, your four hours were up...two minutes ago."

She glared.

Chance smiled.

She kept glaring.

Chance bent and brushed his lips across hers. "I'm fine, baby. I promise."

"You know I was freaked *the fuck* out. Worried out of my mind when you didn't come back. When I couldn't get ahold of you and no one else could either."

He froze, his face going serious. "Cloudless," he murmured. "I—"

Misty cupped his jaw. "I'm only telling you this because I got how you felt," she whispered. "When you told me about how you felt after your dad was hurt, how it felt like the foundation of everything had been shaken."

"Shit, baby, I—"

"No," she said, "I'm not looking for you to apologize, or say anything, or feel guilty. I just—I understood how you felt, and I finally got the uncertainty with your job, that it could be dangerous, and I might lose you and—"

"It's too much."

"No, honey."

"I can take cases that aren't—"

She frowned, sat up, tugging him up with her. "*No, honey.* What you're doing is important, and I think what happened to me illustrates that life happens. It can be dangerous; we could lose people we care about in the blink of an eye." A breath, cupping his jaw again. "What I'm trying to tell you is that even though I was freaked, and I wish I'd called your brother and dad sooner—which I'll do if, God forbid, you turn up missing again—" She narrowed her eyes, warning him without words to not get kidnapped again. Then figured what the hell, she'd warn him aloud, too. "And I'm telling you right now, that better not happen."

"Baby," he said, covering her hands with his.

"I love you. I was worried. I was panicked. I didn't know what the hell I should be doing," she murmured, "and *never once* did I even consider that you wouldn't be walking through the front door of Tangled or into my house or up the driveway of your parents'. Don't you see? I knew you'd come back to me. I knew you'd do *anything* in your power to get *right* here, so much so that I never even considered the possibility otherwise."

His lips parted.

She went on, "So I'm so freaking glad I ran into your car and that you asked me out in front of *everyone*. I'm so glad that we beat Pirate's Booty and you love my cupcakes. I'm glad you're letting me pick out paint colors for your office and you didn't hesitate to move into my house, even though we're still arguing about who's going to pay the bills."

Now his lips began to curve.

"I'll worry," she said. "I know I will. But I also trust you to keep your word," she added when his face fell again. "You told me you're going to make some changes so it's safe, and I believe you. Because you promised to not hurt me again, and you haven't. You promised to call, and you did. You promised to care for me, and you have. And most importantly, you promised to love me, and you have in *every single way* I could have ever hoped for." Her eyes stung; her voice dropped to a whisper. "And that's all I need, baby. I trust you. I trust what you tell me. Because you've proven that I can over and over again."

"Fuck."

She blinked. "What?"

"You're supposed to be the crier."

And then she saw. The tears in the corners of his eyes, gathering on his lashes. "Chance," she said softly.

He reached for her, pulled her close. "I never thought it would be worth it, worth the risk of putting my heart out there. But only because I had no fucking idea it could ever feel like *this*." He leaned back enough to meet her eyes. "It's so big, so wonderful. I swear I should be floating in the sky like I'm strapped to a thousand helium balloons because what I feel for you is *everything*. Every. Fucking. Thing. This"—he slapped a hand to his chest, just above his heart—"beats for you. It was like the first moment I laid eyes on you I knew, *knew* that I would never be the same, and it felt so right, I couldn't even *think* about running from it. I could only stand there and let it come for me. Because you are the fucking love of my life, and I will never *ever* let you go."

"Chance."

His hands were gentle as they smoothed over her skin.

"I think *I'm* going to cry now," she whispered.

He grinned then pulled her close. "Lay it on me, Cloudless."

So she did.

And just like she knew he would, he took all those tears and was unfazed.

And when she was done, left with swollen eyes and a stuffy nose, he produced a box of tissues from somewhere.

Because...he was Chance.

Because...he had her.

And because she had him, too...she wiped his eyes first.

EPILOGUE
CUPCAKE

Chance, Two Months Later

"No," he snapped, smacking Carter's hand away. "These aren't for you."

"Dude," his brother growled, going back and reaching right for the cupcake he couldn't fucking have. "I haven't gotten any yet, and—"

"These aren't for you."

And he tried to communicate what that meant, since his brother fucking knew that he was trying to propose to Misty that evening, along with every other member of his family, including Rob, who hadn't been happy about the rapid speed of their relationship until Chance reminded Rob that he hadn't exactly moved slow with his own sister.

Now, his eyes were wide, his lips pressed flat as he tried to warn Carter off.

But it was Soph who saved the day, mainly because she hissed, "Hey, dumbass, the ring is in there."

"The—" Carter's mouth fell open. "Oh, shit."

"Exactly," she said, but her eyes were amused as she smoothed a hand over her rounded stomach. His niece or nephew was growing like crazy, but Chance was less worried about that at the moment and more concerned about whether Misty had heard the bit about the ring. Which Soph seemed to get, saying, "Mom has her covered out back. Asking about a pattern for a baby blanket."

Chance relaxed.

Because if anyone got Misty talking about knitting, she'd be there for hours.

She *had* been out there for hours.

It was the first time they'd hosted a Jackson Family dinner at Misty's house—well, *his* and Misty's house since he was now on the mortgage and paying for half of the bills (and that had only taken him a dozen arguments...and even more orgasms, but he'd persevered). His family knew the score. Misty's friends knew the score (and yes, they were family now, too). They'd all been cool. They'd all played it relaxed and like it was any other dinner.

But...they were getting antsy.

Case in point Sophie asking, "Ready?" and pairing that with a deliberate look to the back deck.

"No," he muttered, suddenly realizing this was a dumb idea.

He didn't want to do this in front of their family. Fuck, everyone had already had an opinion about where to put the ring, when he should do it.

And for the record, it was his dad's idea for the ring in the cupcake—and he'd even gotten a little plastic container for Chance to shove up through the bottom—hence the plate of wrapper-free cupcakes that Carter wasn't allowed to touch.

Also, Soph had decided at sunset—which was definitely a romantic time of day but also meant he'd had to wait and worry about his proposal *for hours.*

And *everyone* had an opinion on what he should say.

Opinions he'd ignored.

Because this was about him and Misty.

And they were the only ones whose opinion's mattered. Okay, not the *only* ones, but it was their relationship, their hopefully-soon-to-be marriage, and so, in this case, yes, they were the ones that mattered the most.

Also, he was delaying.

A fact he knew because…well, he was delaying, but also because everyone in the room was getting antsy.

As well as everyone on the back deck apparently.

Because Misty chose that exact instant to walk through the door, his mom on her heels and looking regretful.

"Sorry," she mouthed.

"Misty," Frankie said, "I had a question about that stitch…"

"Just a second," Misty told her. "I need to check on dessert."

Rob, trailing the trio, did Chance a solid and tried to get her back outside to the planned proposal location (Soph had positioned a chair right near a rosebush, apparently the floral scent was just *perfect* for a proposal). "I thought you wanted me to give you an estimate on the back fence."

"Later." She waved a hand, eyes coming to Chance. "I thought you were going to bring out…" She trailed off.

Probably because their kitchen was crammed full of everyone else.

"Is everything okay?" she asked, drawing the question out, her gaze moving out of the room.

"Everything's fine," Soph said. "We were all just trying to get our hands on your cupcakes, but Chance was fending us off so we could eat outside."

Misty frowned and strode toward him. "Well, that's silly," she said. "You're pregnant, you get to have as many cupcakes as you want. Here, just take—" She reached for one of the cupcakes on the plate Chance was holding.

"No!"

Nine voices—five brothers (including Rob), one sister, one friend, one set of parents—spoke at once.

Not surprisingly, Misty froze.

Chance, for his part, was struggling to find the words.

"Okay," she said slowly. "What's going on?"

Soph glanced at him, widening her eyes, and then probably realized he was a lost cause because she huffed out a breath. "It's just really pretty outside and—"

Chance plunked the plate on the counter, shoved his hand into the cupcake, and snatched out the ring.

Chocolate went *everywhere*.

But he hardly noticed.

Because he was blurting, "Will you marry me?"

Or rather shouting it.

Literally *shouting* it, making everyone in the kitchen jump, including Misty.

He held up his hand, covered in frosting and cake crumbs and holding a disgusting-looking ring holder.

Soph recovered first.

She snatched the ring holder out of his hand and moved to the sink.

Carter was second.

He handed Chance a dish towel to clean up.

Rob was third.

He grabbed the plate of cupcakes—most of them, honestly, worse for wear—and led the procession out of the kitchen.

Except for Carter, who actually had to pause by his side and wipe his hand.

And Soph, who then plunked the now-freed ring into his hand with a sigh.

Then they were gone, the door closed behind them.

"Did you ask what I thought you did?" Misty whispered.

Chance nodded. "Turned out the proposal in front of our family meant I panicked."

She held up her thumb and pointer finger, barely an inch apart. "Just a little bit." But she was smiling. "You want to get married?"

Another nod, and fuck, why couldn't he find all the words

he'd practiced? Everything he'd wanted to give to her. He just stood there like an idiot, with the ring in his palm and his eyes marking every feature of her face.

"I bet you had it all planned out, didn't you?" Her smile grew. "The cupcake. The chair that Soph insisted I sit in by the roses—which smell great, by the way, but are full of bees."

He winced.

She moved toward him, body melting against him, her hand resting on his chest. "You want to make things official?"

"I want you in my life forever."

Her lips parted. Her eyes went glassy.

And finally, he got his shit together.

He gave her all the things he'd practiced, everything she deserved to hear. All the love he had in his heart for her. And then he got down on one knee and asked (not yelled), "Will you marry me?"

Tears ran down her face.

She nodded.

She pushed out a broken, "Y-yes."

He slipped the ring on her finger…and then he pulled out the wad of tissue from his pocket.

And wiped her eyes.

And then, *then* he kissed her, knowing that his life had only changed for the better when Misty Hansen had crashed into his car.

Because she'd given him absolutely everything.

Fun. Fucking. Friends.

And…forever.

———

Carter

The sound of retching drew him from the back deck and into the guest bathroom.

Maggie was bent over the toilet, face pale and her brown curls stuck to her face. Her eyes came to his, seeming to sense him opening the door, though she'd been puking loudly, and he'd been intentionally quiet. "I—" She broke off, lost her dinner in the toilet again.

Fuck.

It had been months of this now.

Months of her puking.

Months of her losing weight when she was supposed to be gaining it.

He reached into the linen closet and pulled out a towel, wetting it at the faucet and squeezing out the excess, so the material was merely damp when he placed it on the back of her neck.

She moaned quietly. "I'm—"

And then she went again, christening the porcelain goddess.

"Don't try to talk," he murmured, running a hand up and down her back, feeling the bumps of her spine. Fuck, she'd lost a lot of weight.

"Did—" Retch. "I—" Retch. "Miss it?"

"The proposal?"

A nod.

"She said yes."

"Shit," Maggie muttered, resting her head on the toilet seat, which probably wasn't the most sanitary thing, but she'd stopped vomiting for the moment, so Carter sure as hell wasn't going to say anything.

"She'll understand."

Everyone would.

There was no hiding Maggie's pregnancy—not with the constant vomiting and the weight loss—and even if he hadn't moved to town and spent lots of time with Misty and her crew, and that crew hadn't spent lots of time at his parents' and Rob and Soph's house—meaning that Carter ended up spending lots of time with Maggie, Raven, and Frankie, as well as his own family—he still would have noticed.

Because it was awful.

Soph was the picture of a glowing, easy pregnancy.

Maggie was the picture of suffering.

If he didn't have the example of Soph, he'd wonder why women would go through the hell Maggie was facing.

Maggie started to push to her feet, wavered.

He caught her arm. "What are you doing?"

"I need to go apologize," she said, still too damned pale, "and tell them congratulations and—"

"You need to sit down before you pass out," he ordered, pushing her down, and it spoke for how weak she must be feeling, because she didn't argue, just sat on the bathmat and leaned against the wall.

He gave her that for a few minutes, and when it seemed like the vomiting had stopped, at least for the moment, he reached into his pocket and pulled out what he'd bought the other day.

A ginger hard candy.

"Here," he said, handing it to her. "It's supposed to settle your stomach," he told her when she just stared at it in her palm.

"I—"

He reached into his other pocket, pulled out something he'd decided to start keeping there.

A fresh toothbrush.

He'd bought a jumbo-sized box of them online, promising to keep one on him at all times. Because Maggie always wanted to brush her teeth afterward. Which he got. Because who wanted to taste their sick?

He wasn't thinking about why he'd done that.

Or bought the candy.

Or had promised himself to be carrying them at all times.

He already knew.

Knew the moment she'd called him *Mr. Sexy Carter Jackson*.
Knew when she'd asked him to *wreck* her.

Maggie Augustin was special.

She had spark.

She was gorgeous and curvy and smart.

She was going to be his.

But he'd been seeing someone else, and it wasn't easy to break things off with Anika. Not only because his ex was good in bed, but because they'd just moved in together and he'd thought things were progressing toward something permanent.

Except, then he'd seen his brother with Misty.

And he'd known that Anika wasn't even in the realm of a woman like Misty.

A woman like Maggie.

But Maggie was pregnant, and the kid wasn't his, and she was sick all the time, and she was trying to figure out her life as a single parent.

And…it wasn't the time to make a move.

Still, she needed someone to look out for her. Which was why he held out the toothbrush—and the tiny packet of toothpaste (same brand as he'd seen her carry in her purse)—and asked, "Unless you'd rather brush your teeth first?"

Her mouth fell open. "Why are you—"

He didn't want to answer any questions that began with why. So, he slipped an arm under hers, tugged her to her feet, and stood by her as she brushed her teeth. Then he nodded to the candy. "Want to try it?"

He'd read online that peppermint and ginger might help.

Hopefully the mint from the toothpaste along with the candy would do the trick.

Her fingers shook as she opened the wrapper. After a moment of hesitation, she popped it into her mouth.

They both stood there in silence as she sucked the candy.

Waiting for her to either blow or for her stomach to settle.

The latter happened.

She pressed her hand flat to her abdomen, and astonished eyes met his. "I feel better," she breathed. "I actually *feel better.*"

"Good, Curls. I'm glad it helped."

Wide eyes met his. "Why are you being nice to me?"

Another question that began with why that he didn't want to answer.

"I'm nice to everyone."

That was true. He was a nice guy.

"To the point of carrying ginger candies and toothbrushes?"

And toothpaste, not that he was going to say that.

"Yes."

"Liar." She started to push by him, but even with the toothpaste and the candy, she was still pale and a little shaky. He caught her, steadied her again. "You just feel sorry for me."

"You're right, I do."

She lurched back like he'd slapped her.

"Right," she said, eyes glistening. "Feel sorry for the stupid girl who got pregnant accidentally, whose baby daddy told her to get rid of it, and when she didn't, happily signed his rights away. Before my first doctor's appointment. I get it. I *was* stupid. I got knocked up by a loser who didn't even know how to please a woman, and now I'm pregnant and alone and *so fucking stupid.*" She sniffed. "I don't know what the fuck I'm thinking. I can't do this. I can't have this baby—"

She clamped a hand to her mouth again.

Carter'd had enough.

He gripped her shoulders, shook her lightly, and bent so his face was in hers. "Breathe, Maggie."

"I—"

Another jostle.

"Breathe."

She breathed.

"Right," he said. "I don't feel sorry for you because you're pregnant. I feel bad for you because you're puking your guts up every second. I feel sorry that the sperm donor is such a moron that he isn't going to be in the baby's life—though that's probably for the best, since no man worth his salt would do that." He took a breath, gentled his voice. "And you're not alone. You have us. *All* of us. You can do this, and I'll help you. *We'll* help you."

A sniff.

More glistening.

"I still don't know why you're being so nice."

He slid his hand up from her shoulder, cupped her cheek. "Don't you?"

And he forgot all about it being a horrible time to make a move, all about her being vulnerable and him not wanting to take advantage.

Carter only thought of this woman in front of him, scared and alone and so damned beautiful it made his teeth ache. She needed him. Not at some indefinite point in the future. But now. *Right now.* She just shook her head and stared up at him.

"I like you, Maggie. You're beautiful and funny and kind." He stroked a finger over her cheek. "I like you a lot and—"

She gagged, spun out of his hold, and barely made it to the toilet in time.

Perfect.

He'd expressed his interest.

She could barely contain the vomit.

Luckily, he had another toothbrush in his pocket.

———

THANK YOU FOR READING! I hope you loved meeting Misty and Chance! The next book in the Life Sucks series is FUBAR. **She was pregnant and alone...and sick.**

CLICK HERE TO READ FUBAR NOW>

And if you enjoyed Train Wreck, you'll love the sexy, sweet, and close-knit Breakers Hockey crew. The first book in the series, BROKEN, is now live!

It is sexy, hot, adorable and such a fun read. You will not be able to put this down!" —Amazon Reviewer

———

I so appreciate your help in spreading the word about my books, including sharing with friends! Please leave a review on your favorite book site!

If you'd like to receive emails from me for new releases and monthly giveaway sign up for my newsletter at https://www.elisefaber.com/newsletter.

You can also join my Facebook group, the Fabinators, for exclusive giveaways and sneak peeks of future books.

———

Want a free bonus story? Hate missing Elise's new releases?
Love contests, exclusive excerpts and giveaways?
Then signup for Elise's newsletter here!
https://www.elisefaber.com/newsletter

———

And join Elise's fan group, the Fabinators https://www.
facebook.com/groups/fabinators for insider information, sneak
peaks at new releases, and fun freebies! Hope to see you there!

LIFE SUCKS SERIES

ALSO BY ELISE FABER

Centered

Charging

Caged

Crashed

A Gold Christmas

Cycled

Caught

Cap

Covered

Breakers Hockey (all stand alone)

Broken

Boldly

Breathless

Ballsy

Bewitched

Blowout

Rush Hockey Trilogy

Big Puck Energy

Filthy Puckboy

So Pucking Over It

Love, Action, Camera (all stand alone)

Dotted Line

Action Shot

Close-Up

End Scene

Meet Cute

Love After Midnight **(all stand alone)**

Rum And Notes

Virgin Daiquiri

On The Rocks

Sex On The Seats

Life Sucks Series (all stand alone)

Train Wreck

Hot Mess

Dumpster Fire

Clusterf*@k

FUBAR

Perfect Storm

Free Fallx

Roosevelt Ranch Series (all stand alone, series complete)

Disaster at Roosevelt Ranch

Heartbreak at Roosevelt Ranch

Collision at Roosevelt Ranch

Regret at Roosevelt Ranch

Desire at Roosevelt Ranch

Phoenix Series (read in order)

Phoenix Rising

Dark Phoenix

Phoenix Freed

Phoenix: LexTal Chronicles (rereleasing soon, stand alone, Phoenix world)

From Ashes

In Flames

To Smoke

KTS Series (all stand alone, series complete)

Riding The Edge

Crossing The Line

Leveling The Field

Scorching The Earth

Cocky Heroes World

Tattooed Troublemaker

ABOUT THE AUTHOR

USA Today bestselling author, Elise Faber, loves chocolate, Star Wars, Harry Potter, and hockey (the order depending on the day and how well her team -- the Sharks! -- are playing). She and her husband also play as much hockey as they can squeeze into their schedules, so much so that their typical date night is spent on the ice. Elise changes her hair color more often than some people change their socks, loves sparkly things, and is the mom to two exuberant boys. She lives in Northern California. Connect with her in her Facebook group, the Fabinators or find more information about her books at www.elisefaber.com.

    f facebook.com/elisefaberauthor

    a amazon.com/author/elisefaber

    BB bookbub.com/profile/elise-faber

    O instagram.com/elisefaber

    g goodreads.com/elisefaber

    p pinterest.com/elisefaberwrite